DA
CORNER

JAMAR JENKINS

This Book is dedicated to my heavenly angel, my mother Leontine Jenkins.

Table of Contents

Chapter 1

Manny and his crew were sitting on the stoop, across the street, watching Miguel serve car after car as he stood on the corner. Man, that nigga getting money Lil Sam said, one of Manny's closest friends. I swear Manny agreed. We need to holla at him and see if he needs some security or something. You think a nigga like Miguel ain't got some muthafuka's watching his back already, Manny replied. I mean like, look out for the Law, Alex said. Shidd ask'em, Manny replied. Nigga you the one be running errands for'em and shit, you ask'em, Lil Sam, joined in. Nah I'm cool, Manny Said. You nigga's came up with the idea, so you go tell'em, Manny snapped. Aye, Manny. Miguel yelled from the corner. What's up, Manny replied? Check it out real quick! Manny jumped up from the stoop and walked over to where Miguel was at. What's up? Run to the set store for me and grab a box of baggies and a razor blade, Miguel said. Aight! Miguel tried to hand Manny a $5 bill but Manny rejected it. I got you. Manny said as he marched to the Jet Store.

As Manny returned and approached Miguel with the bag, he saw that Miguel was in a deep conver-sation with someone who had to be a chick on the phone, because he was smiling from ear to ear. Miguel waved his hand at Manny telling him to hold on. Manny sat on the fire hydrant waiting for Miguel to finish caking. Aight! Lil Homie, my bad, Miguel said. Naw it's all good. Here tho manny said handing Miguel the bag, then walked off. Aye Manny, Miguel said, don't go anywhere I need you and the crew to hold the corner down while I go handle some business real quick. Aight! Manny said. As he walked back to the stoop where Alex and Lil Sam was. Aye, Miguel just told me don't go anywhere, he wants us to hold the block down for'em till he comes back, for real? Alex said getting pumped up, hell yea, Manny replied. Yoo, Miguel said waving Manny and his crew over to the corner, What's up Miguel? Look man, I need y'all Lil niggas to hold it down till I come back, I'm about to go fuck with this bitch for about an hour, no longer than 2 Miguel said. Everything already took care of, all y'all gotta do is get the money from the hype's and send'em to ya homie, he gonna give'em the product. That way if the Law comes, they don't know shit, Miguel explained. Now Manny you orchestrate who gone do what, I'll be back in a minute, Miguel said, as he gave Manny the jab and the phone, hold it down, y'all do good then we can make this a permanent thing, Miguel said. Aight, Alex you look out for the Law, Lil Sam, you serve the hypes and I'll collect the bread, Manny said. Aight let's get to it then, Alex said as the hypes started coming from every direction. Damn, this bitch rocking, Lil Sam said to Manny. I know right. I can even fit all this money in my pocket, Manny said. What you got left anyway, Manny asked, shidd only one jab left, Lil Sam Said. A jab, that's only 13 bags. Aw, that shit finna be gone, where the fuck, Miguel at? 2 hours had come and gone and Alex had to get home soon because his uncle would kick his ass if he was a minute past his curfew, which was 7:00 and it was 6:50.

The trap phone had rung and it was a hype asking for a jab. Aight, hurry cause that's all that's left, first come, first serve, Manny, said, hanging up. Not even 5 minutes had passed and the hype that called was turning the corner on a 10-speed bike. Hey come on man, where's Miguel at, the hype said, Miguel ain't around right now, Manny said, directing the hype to Lil Sam. The hype walked up to Lil Sam examining the jab making sure it was no bullshit. Aight, Shorty here the hype said handing Lil Sam the money. Naw that go to him Sam said, pointing to Manny. The hype gave the bread to Manny and rode off. That's it right there Lil Sam said, ain't shit else. I know where's the fuck is Miguel at Man? Manny said, getting frustrated. Aye, Alex yelled. I gotta go man it's already past my curfew. Yall finna get my ass kicked, Alex said, getting off the stoop heading towards his crib. Aight, we'll see you tomorrow. This nigga Miguel tweaking, Lil Sam said. Lil Sam and Manny didn't have a curfew, shidd they didn't have parents. Both their mothers were crackheads and their fathers weren't around either, so they were out here.

Manny and Alex sat on the stoop waiting for Miguel to come back. It was now 8:30 pm when Manny saw the headlights of a car coming down the street, he stood up to see if it was Miguel in his G8 when he heard the pipes growling he knew it was Miguel pulling up on the corner, he killed the engine, then jumped out. What up my niggas? Miguel said with a kool-aid smile on his face. Nigga you said an hour or 2. Yo ass, been gone since 4:00 and it' 8:40 man, Manny snapped. My bad Lil bro, the bitch wouldn't let a nigga leave, Miguel said. That was Miguel's problem, chasing bitches, instead of chasing money. Man, it's money ova bitches, Lil Sam said, as he stood up. Yea aight Lil nigga, once you start fucking you'll see, Miguel said. What y'all got left tho? Shit, man, we sold out around 5:00

nigga, Manny said. Damn, I'm tripping, Miguel said. That's what we telling you, Manny snapped, handing Miguel the money. Miguel counted the money to make sure that it was all there, and it was. $1300 for 10 jabs. Miguel piled off 3 hundred dollar bills and gave them to Manny, that's for you and the crew, Miguel said. Manny's eyes were big ass golf balls, thanks Miguel, Manny said, anytime you need us let me know. Y'all come thru tomorrow around 9 am, I got something for y'all, Miguel said, getting in the car and pulling off.

Chapter 2

Alex, Manny, and Lil Sam all stayed in the same building on 39th & State. Manny decided to stop by Alex's crib and give him his cut, but when they got off the elevator they heard Alex Uncle in there going off on Alex. Damn man, I wish I could kill him, Manny said. Come on man we'll give him his curve tomorrow, if we see him Lil Sam said. Alex and his sister, who was 2 years older than him, had been living with their uncle ever since their parents died in a fire. So, their uncle got custody of them, he kept all the Government checks and blew them on liquor and cocaine. When he was drunk and high he would creep into Alex's sister's Alexandria's room and have his way with her. Alexandria was only 17 years old, but she had a grown woman's body. Her breast was too big for her bra, she was a double D and her panties were at least 3 sizes too small. In the years that they stayed with their uncle, every other night he snuck into her room and made her have sex with him. Alexandria was a straight-A student, but by not having any clothes and not being able to get her hair done, she had a hard time at school. She was always getting picked on because of her clothes and her nappy hair. On top of that, getting innocents taken from her at the young age of 10 years old, She didn't know what to do.

Alex knew what was going on but, what could he do, he couldn't go to the police, because they would send them to DCFS and split them up. Alex vowed to himself that one day he would kill his uncle and this nightmare would be over with. Claude had just kicked Alex's ass not because he was late, but because he interrupted him from getting his dick sucked by Alexandria. When Alex walked into the room and saw Claude forcing his dick down Alexandria's throat he charged, Claude throwing useless punches. Claude turned around and punched

Alex square in his chest, knocking the wind out of him. From there he stomped Alex out, kicking him everywhere except the head. Lil muthafucka, you wanna be captain save a hoe, huh, I'll show you Claude shouted as he beat the fuck outta Alex until he was tired. After he was done with Alex he went back into the room with Alexandria. She was curled up under the blanket scared of what Claude had just done to Alex, so when her room door opened, she knew what was next. Claude walked up to her and snatched the sheet off her, exposing her teenage body he pulled her by both legs, ripped her small panties off, pulled his dick out, and plunged into her like she was a grown woman. Alexandria laid there emotionless as Claude pounded away. Alex laid on the floor in the front room beat up, crying his eyes out, with the sweet taste of revenge on his mind.

Chapter 3

The next morning, Manny got up at 7:00 am. He was geeked up about the possibility of being a worker for Miguel that he couldn't sleep. He brushed his teeth and washed his face, then threw yesterday's, jogging suit on. As he was about to walk out the door, he noticed his mother sleep on the couch, next to some random nigga. Aye, Aye, Famo, Manny said tapping the stranger. You gotta get the fuck outta here, Manny yelled, waking his mother up also. You better watch your mouth, Manny. This man is old enough to be your daddy. But he ain't, Manny said, waving his mom off, directing his attention back to the stranger. Let's ride fool, Manny said, holding the door open for the guy to walk out. As the guy walked out the door, Manny was right behind him,

Aye, don't make that a habit, Manny said, as he walked to Lil Sam's crib. I'm good youngster, I just needed a place to crash last night, the guy said, as he hopped on the elevator.

I'm getting tired of this shit, Manny said to himself, as he knocked on Lil Sam's door. Lil Sam's mother Tracy opened the door wide open, in her panties, looking like shit. Wassup Manny? She said looking him up and down. Nothing, is Lil Sam woke yet, Manny asked? Sam, manny out here, Tracy yelled. Come on in she said as she turned around walking off. You could tell back in the day that Tracy was bad because she still had some features. Her ass was still fat and her hair was still long and curly. Manny got caught up in a daze looking at her ass jiggle in what use to be white, but now yellow panties. Nigga, Lil Sam said coming out of the bathroom catching Manny staring at his mom's ass. Wassup Boi? Manny said. You ready man he added. Yea Lil Sam said. Ma you need to put some clothes on when my homies come over too, Lil Sam snapped, boy shut the fuck up, I'm grown, Manny can see these goodies, it ain't like he can handle all this ass anyway, Tracy said pissing Lil Sam off as he and Manny left out. That bitch starting to blow me, bro, for real, Lil Sam said. She ain't worse than my O.G., Manny said, as they walked down the stairs to Alex Crib.

When they got to Alex's floor he was already in the hallway. Fuck you going? Lil Sam asked, getting away from this muthafucka, Alex said. I already know, Manny said. Here, Manny gave Alex the hundred that Miguel gave them. Damn all this for looking out, Alex said. Hell yea, Manny replied, he got some more work for us today at 9:00, he wants us on the corner, so let's go nigga. The trio jumped on the elevator and got off on the ground level. We heard unc bitch ass in there last night, Manny said. Alex just shook his head, I'm getting tired of that shit, Alex snapped. What you gonna do? Manny asked. I' ma kill his ass, Alex said, Kill'em and then what are you gonna do? DCFS gonna take yall, Lil Sam Said. I don't give a fuck, I'll think of something, Alex said. Let's tell Miguel, see if he can help us out. I'm quite sure Miguel knows him, the nigga getting high anyway. Anybody around here getting high copping from Miguel, Manny Said. Aight let's see what he says, Alex replied.

As they got to the stoop, about 10 minutes after they got there, Miguel pulled up. What's up with my Lil niggas? He Said, jumping outta the car. Shit man tryna get this paper, Manny said. I see, Miguel replied. Check this out tho! We gone run this shit the same way, we did yesterday, but the difference is this, Miguel said, pulling out the Draco. Whoever doing lookout gonna have the pole on'em in case a nigga think it's sweet. I' ma give yall 50 jabs each one is 13, y'all take 30 off each one. So when the bundle is gone, y'all split 1500 apiece, cool Miguel asked. Hell yea the trio said in unison. It's gone do that on a light day, on a good day it does every bit of 5 -50 bundles so that 7,500 y'all can split. Manny's eyes got big as fuck, when he heard that. Here, Miguel said, handing each one of'em nex-tel chirps. Y'all know how to chirp right, Miguel asked. Hell yea, Lil Sam replied, aight then, yall can switch it up on how y'all gonna do it as far as who is serving, collecting, and watching out. The fiends should start coming through in the next 20 minutes. They know the shop opens at 9 Am, Miguel said, walking off.

Aye, Alex called out after Miguel, What's up, Miguel replied. I need to holla at you, Alex said, walking up to him. Alex explained to him what Claude was doing to him and his sister and Miguel was livid at what he just heard. That nigga looks like his head was about to pop, Manny said, to Lil Sam. I swear it does, Lil Sam replied. Miguel got into the G8 and snatched off. Alex walked back up to Manny and Lil Sam with a smile on his face. You told him Lil Sam asked, yea Alex replied, what he say? Manny asked, shidd, that he gone take care of it, Alex replied. Aw ok. Who doing lookout Manny? Asked. Alex was so thirsty to hold the gun that he volunteered. Give it to me, Alex said, Snatching the gun from Manny. Aight then, I'll serve and you collect today. Manny said to Lil Sam and we'll switch up every day. Shid y'all switch up, I'm holding this bitch every day, Alex said. Manny and

Lil Sam Laughed as they went and posted up on the corner waiting for the hypes to come. That morning rush was crazy. Manny was damn near thru half of the bundles and it wasn't even noon yet. Man, it's only 15 jabs left Manny told Lil Sam. This must be one of them good days, Miguel was talking about Lil Sam replied, hell yea Manny agreed, lights out, Alex yelled, that means the Law was coming. Alex stepped into the hallway and Manny and Lil Sam scattered up the block. Manny had crossed the street so if they hopped out, he wouldn't be by the bundle. By them being so young and small the Law rode right past them. Alex came through the chirp, they gone yet? yea Lil Sam said as he turned around. Alex came back out and Manny went back across the street. By 2:00 the whole bundle was gone. Manny had to call Miguel for a re-up. We out, Manny said through the phone. Say less, Miguel replied. 10 minutes later Miguel was pulling up with another 50 bundles, here that should do it for the day. You know after 5:00 we shut down, Miguel said. Aight, Manny replied, as he took the jab. By 4:45 that bundle was gone the trio had made a total of $1000 each on their 1st day of work.

When Miguel pulled up, it looked like he had been in a scuffle, his shirt was wrinkled with a Lil blood on it too. You good, Manny said, as he jumped into the passenger seat to give Miguel the money. Yea, I'm straight, Yo tell Lil man Alex his problem ova with, You niggas finna be making enough money to provide for ya' self anyway, Miguel said. Yall keep the pole too, Miguel said, about to pull off. Aw yea, I'm picking you up in the morning around 7 AM so be on point, Miguel told Manny as he pulled off.

Chapter 4

Man, I can't wait till tomorrow, Lil Sam said as the trio walked up to their building. Can you believe we made a G apiece in one day, Alex said, hell naw, Lil Sam replied. I hope every other day is a good day too, Alex said. Aye tho, I wonder what Miguel did to Claude's bitch ass. He said I ain't gone have to worry about him no more. He probably beat his ass, Manny said, or killed him, Lil Sam chimed in. Nah, I don't think he would do some shit like that, Miguel doesn't look like the type, Alex said. Shid, you must didn't see the look in that nigga eyes, Manny said, as they walked into the building. Well, I'm about to see when I walk through this door, Alex said, as they all went their separate ways, once the elevator arrived. Lil Sam and Manny stayed right down the hall from each other, so they got off 1st on the 13th floor, Aight, they said to Alex when the door closed. Aye Lil Sam, Miguel said he gonna come scoop me up in the AM so I'll hit y'all when I get done with him, Manny said, as Lil Sam opened his door.

When Lil Sam opened the door he noticed that the crib was halfway clean. Lil Sam went to the refrigerator, grabbed a pop, and sat on the couch. Where the fuck my O.G. at, Lil Sam thought to himself. Right then he heard moaning coming from the back room. What the fuck, he said to himself as he got up from the couch, as he got closer to the bedroom door, he heard the moaning getting louder so he opened the door and saw his mom bent over the bed getting her brains beat in by a nigga that looked to be Lil Sam's age. What the fuck is going on in here, Lil Sam shouted, startling the dude, get the fuck outta my room, Tracy said to Sam, I pay the bills around here she said. Don't stop, put that dick back in, Tracy, told the nigga who had to have given her a bag to fuck. Lil Sam closed the door and went into his room….

Meanwhile, Manny was in his crib alone, with no food or company, Damn it ain't never shit to eat in here, Manny said to himself. I can't wait till I get my bread up and get the fuck away from here. Manny grabbed the menu from the pizza place off the couch and ordered a large pizza, then turned the TV on to see what was on. Alexandria, Alex said walking into the crib, yea, she said walking out the backroom in her robe. You here alone? Alex said, yea, I have been here by myself all day, she replied. Where the fuck, Claude at? Alex thought to himself. You ate something yet Alex asked his big sister? No, I haven't eaten all day, she said. You want some pizza, Alex asked? Yea, but who got money for that, Alexandria asked? Don't worry about that, he replied, things about to change around here, Alex said, handing his sister the Draco, what are you doing with that Alexandria said. Man be cool and put that in the ceiling in your room, Alex snapped. Also here, Alex said, going into his pocket grabbing the money he just made. Take 400 for yourself and go get your hair done and by yourself some outfits and shit.

Stash the rest for me ok, Alex told her. Alright, thank you brother, Alexandria said as she went to put the money and gun up.

Chapter 5

The next morning, Miguel was in front of Manny's building at 6:00 am. Let's do it, Miguel said thru the chirp, Aight, I'm coming out right now. Manny said. A few seconds later Manny was coming out the project doors, walking up to the car. What's da word, Lil homie? Miguel said as Manny got into the car. Shit man, tryna get like you, Manny said. Naw get better than me Miguel replied. So where are we going? Finna show you something, Miguel said. About 30 minutes later they were pulling up to a complex building on the north side. Come on, Miguel said. As they parked and got out, they walked into the building, Miguel nodded at the lady in the lobby and jumped on the elevator. The door opened up on the 23rd floor, they got off and walked down the hallway to apartment 3C. Miguel opened the door and Manny was amazed at what he saw. Miguel had an all-white sectional couch, 70" TV on the wall, floor-to-ceiling windows overlooking Lake Michigan, and an aquarium filled with fish. Damn this bitch ace, Manny said. I know right one day your shit gonna be better than mine, Miguel said. I'm already encouraged, Manny replied. So why you bring me to your crib? Manny asked, Because I wanna give you something, Miguel went to the back, grabbed a bag, and came back. He emptied the contents on the floor and at least 2 bricks in bundles came falling out. Damn you holding fool, Manny said., that ain't shit, we tryna get a hundred of them thangs, Miguel said, referring to bricks. Look, you grab what you think y'all gonna move this week and you put that shit up at Alex's crib, in the back of Manny's mind, he was wondering why put it at Alex's crib, but he just went with the flow.

Aight, we moved 2 (50) bundles yesterday, so I'll just take 15 (50) bundles that'll be 2 a day and we'll have one leftover just in case, Manny said. See that's why I like you, Miguel said, you be on point, and if y'all run out just hit my line and I got y'all, Miguel said. Aight Manny replied as he grabbed the bundles and headed for the door. Miguel put the bag up in the back and followed Manny to the elevator. Once they were in the car Miguel grabbed the bag from Manny and put it in his stash.. 30 minutes later they were back in front of Manny's building. Aight, Lil nigga, you know the block opens up at 9:00, It's 8 right now, take out what y'all need and put the rest up, Miguel said. I know at Alex's crib, Manny laughed as he got out of the car. HML when y'all on the block so I can come thru, Miguel said as he pulled off.

Manny ran into the building and went straight to Alex's crib. Boom, Boom, Boom, Manny banged on Alex's door. Who is it? Alexandria said, Manny. Alexandria opens the door in her robe, letting Manny in. Hey Manny, she had liked Manny ever since they came to live with Claude. Manny never looked at her like that because of Alex, they were like brothers. Wassup A, Manny said. Where yo brother? Manny said, aw he still sleep Alexandria said opening her robe to give Manny a preview of her goodies. Damn Manny said to himself as he looked at Alexandria's, huge titties and hairy pussy. She had sprouted everywhere, being that her uncle had been making her have sex with him since she was 12. She had been advanced in every way. You are so scary she said to Manny, It wasn't that he was scared, he was on business right now, but he sure would take a rain check tho. Naw, I'll see what's to you, Manny said, licking his lips. He walked past her and went to Alex's room waking him up, get yo ass up, Manny said, kicking Alex, aight man damn, Alex said getting up off the floor. Look, Miguel gave me this, this morning. He told me to stash it here, take out what we gonna need for the day, and put the rest up, where the fuck is ya hype ass uncle, Manny asked? Shidd I don't know the nigga ain't come home last night. Who gives a fuck tho, Alex replied. Manny chirped Lil Sam and told him to come down to Alex's crib, so they could get ready to go open up the corner. So, what we taking with us,

Alex said. Shidd at least 3, we never know how this bitch gonna do today, I'm tryna turn up, you know my Bday next month, Manny said. Aight let me get ready, Alex said as he went into the bathroom.

Manny went and sat on the couch while Alex showered. Alexandria came walking back into the front room this time without a robe on, just panties, no bra. She knew that Alex was in the shower, and it would let her know when he was getting out because you could hear the water drain out. She stood right in front of Manny, Manny wrapped his arms around her, palming her ass then stuck his finger in her pussy, wiggled it around, and pulled it out. Alexandria had juices coming down her leg. Ohh why you stop, she said. Cuz I gotta go, I'll get with you. Manny said. She grabbed his dick as she walked off, you better before it's too late, Alexandria said as she went into her room. Alex came out of the bathroom 5 minutes later and went into his room to put his clothes on. There was a knock at the door, moments later, Manny checked the door and it was Lil Sam, it took you long enough, Manny said.

Nigga fuk you, Lil Sam replied, taking a seat. Miguel scooped me this morning and loaded us up on the work, Manny said. Aw yea, where it's at? Lil Sam asked it's tucked off. We're gonna run through these 3 bundles first, Manny threw them on the table and Alex got the rest put up, Manny said. Aight cool, Lil Sam said as Alex came walking out the back. Y'all ready Alex said, duh nigga Lil sam said. Let's do it then, Alex said, tucking the Draco into his pants as the trio walked out the door. Aye Manny, Alex said once they were on the elevator you bet not fuck my sister, the whole elevator bust out laughing. Forreal tho, I know she likes you tho, I rather it be you than anybody else, Alex explained. I already know, Manny said as they got off the elevator.

The trio walked down the street, around the corner, and was on time to open up the block. We already know you holding the pole Alex, Lil Sam said, so it's my turn to serve he told Manny. Today was even better than the other day. They sold 2 bundles before noon and were working on the 3rd.

Alex had to run back to the crib to grab 2 more bundles. I don't know what Miguel is doing to this shit, but I hope it stays this way Manny said. Lights out! Alex yelled as he stepped into the hallway, 3 transformers pulled up and jumped out on Lil Sam and Manny. What the fuck yall doing on this corner? The white slick boy said. Shit, we waiting for our homie to come so we can go to the gym, Manny said, hoping they don't search him, Manny had at least $8500 on him. Yea! The detective walked around tryna see if anything was outta place. Aight then you lil bastards be careful out here, there's a lot of shooting going on, he said as the 3 trucks pulled off. Damn, I'm glad they ain't search me, I got all this damn money on me, Manny said. Alex, I'm finna give you this money real quick, Manny said, as he jogged across the street and gave Alex the money. Damn, it's 3:30, we need to sell the rest of these bags, Manny said to Lil Sam. What's left, Sam asked? A half bundle (25) jabs. Aw, we should be good by 5:00, Lil Sam said. That's $3,000 in 2 days, Lil Sam said geeked. Yea, Imagine what

Miguel is making tho! On my life, Lil Sam agreed as a crowd of hypes came surrounding him. By 5:00 they had sold 5 bundles, and their day was over. Call the nigga Miguel, Lil Sam said. I did the nigga ain't answer, never mind this him right here, calling me back. Yo, Manny yelled into the phone. He about to pull up, Manny said. 20 minutes later Miguel was pulling up. He jumped out and dapped Manny and Lil Sam up, then saluted Alex in the cut. Man, y'all Lil niggas finna get a raise, Miguel said. That's what I'm saying, Lil Sam replied. We have been running through this shit. Aight, look man I'm giving y'all a free bundle to split that's $1500 fa y'all, Miguel said. Aight cool, Manny replied handing Miguel his money. Naw put it in the armrest, don't do that in public, you don't know who's watching, Miguel said. As Manny went to put the money in the armrest, 2 slick boys pulled up in crown vics, one in the front and one in the back of Miguel G8. Mr. Miguel the black one said, pushing Miguel up against the wall. You mutha-fucka's don't get enough huh. I ain't got shit, pussies damn, Miguel said. Aw, we ain't here for no drugs the white cop said. Somebody must don't like you, you know that body we just found about an hour ago. We gotta live talking witnesses that say they saw you stab the man up and run off. Nah, couldn't have been me. I was right here all yesterday, Miguel said. I bet you were, the cop replied. We will sort this out down at the station, see if they can pick you outta a line-up, the cop said. Aye, Manny gets the keys outta my car and move it, I'll be out in the morning. No, he won't, the white cop said as they threw Miguel in the car and pulled off.

What the fuck, Manny said? Shidd probably Claude, Lil Sam said. You saw that nigga face when Alex was telling him that shit. Probably was, I hope it was, Alex said, how are we gonna move the care tho? That's one thing that pussy taught me how to do, Alex said, drive. Let me see you drive then, Manny said, surprisingly Alex jumped, threw the car into gear, and drove around the block. Damn that nigga do know how to drive, Manny said, as Alex came back around the block. Come on niggas, Alex said, stopping in the middle of the street. Lil Sam and Manny jumped in as Alex turned corner after corner. What if they don't let Miguel out? Then what? Lil Sam said, shid we gotta think of something, Manny replied, that money in the armrest, Manny lifted the armrest and grabbed the $5,000 out as they headed into the building. The trio got on the elevator and went to Alex's crib. They ordered a pizza and talked about their next move if Miguel got charged. Boom, boom, boom, who the fuck is that Alex said, walking to the door, as he looked out the peephole, he saw that it was 2 police officers in suits. Alex ran to get his sister so she could talk to them. Alexandria opened the door in her robe, looking like a grown lady. Yes, she said. How are you ma'am the detective, said? Does Claude Anderson live here, yes, he does, Alexandria replied? Well, I'm sorry to inform you, his body was just discovered in an alley on 43rd and Calumet, oh my God, she said, was he any relation to you? Yes, that was my uncle. I'm so sorry ma; am. If you could come down to the morgue to identify the body. So we can declare him that would be fine, the Detective said. Alright, I'll be down as soon as I can, Alexandria said, putting on her best impression of a woman who cared as she closed the door. Her face lit up when she turned around as if she just hit the lottery. You heard them she said to Alex, his ass finally dead, thank you, God, Alexandria said, as she went to her room. I guess Miguel did off the nigga, Manny said. Shid, I guess so, Alex said. We just gotta hope they don't charge Miguel with it. Nigga they wouldn't have come and got him if they weren't gone charge him. We need to find that witness and drop her ass so he can get out. Hell yea, Manny agreed. Just when shit was looking up for us, Lil Sam said, Aw we still good, Manny replied, nigga them 10 bundles gonna be gone then where we gonna get some work from, as good as this shit. We gonna wait until Miguel calls, then I'll let y'all know my plan. It's definitely not over, this shit just getting started, Manny said.

Chapter 6

You have a collect call from Miguel, to accept charges press one. Manny pressed one instantly. Lil Homie, what bro? Manny replied. They tryna stick it to me, they charge me with this bogus ass body, you got my keys right, Miguel asked. Yea, I got'em what you want me to do? Shidd get you a driver to move around in the car unless you know how to drive. My rent paid up for the year at the crib, the keys to the house on the ring, Miguel said, as Manny looked at the keys. You know what to do, Miguel said letting him know that the work was there too, luckily, he just took Manny to his crib. Do yo thang Lil nigga, I'll be calling you tho, y'all put some money on my books, the lawyer already paid. I'll know who the witness is once the trial starts. But with my lawyer I'll know when I get my discovery, Miguel said. Y'all gotta find a way when that's gone or go to the set store, Miguel said, as the phone disconnected. Manny got up and went to Alex's crib, surprisingly the door was open. Alex, Alex, Manny shouted. What, nigga damn, Alex snapped. First off why the fuck is ya door wide open? And why the fuck is you still sleep? Cuz nigga it's 8 am and I'm tired as hell. Nigga we got work to do, the show doesn't stop cause Miguel is gone, Manny snapped. Aight, man Alex said, going to the washroom to get himself together.

Manny got up and opened Alexandria's bedroom door and she was sound asleep. Manny walked in there and kissed her on the forehead. She jumped to the touch of his lips, but when she opened her eyes and saw him, she smiled. Manny then kissed her lips, she pulled him into the bed with her. She was completely naked. Knowing that she didn't have to worry about Claude again, she got comfortable. Manny slid in between her legs with his basketball shorts. Kissing her passionately. Alexandria reached down and pulled his dick out of his shorts, propped her leg up, and slid it right in. Oh shit, she said as Manny grinding in and out of her. Damn, you feel so good, Manny said, Alexandria was in a whole other world as Manny started to pound even harder as he was nearing an orgasm, I'm coming Manny said as he exploded all in Alexandria. Damn baby, that was good, I' ma need some more of that, she said as Manny got up. Manny, Alex yelled out, what's up? Manny responded, walking outta Alexandria room, I told you don't fuck my sister Alex said jokingly, Shid she fucked me, Manny said seriously. Shut up, Alexandria yelled from the bedroom.

Come on man, Alex said, Sam in the front of the building waiting on us. Grab all the jabs, Manny said, Hell naw we gone take 5, we gotta slow stroke em this all we got, Alex said. No, it ain't, I got the key to Miguel's crib he called this morning, he said they were charging him and that he'd be sitting for a while. He said we can have the crib, the rent paid up for the year, we can ride the car too. Then he said something bout hollering at them at the set store, I guess that's who he was getting up with, Manny added. Damn, I feel responsible for that shit, Alex said, if I wouldn't have told him that shit, he wouldn't be booked. All we gotta do is off the witness then he's good, Manny said. How we're gonna know who the witness is, Alex, replied, Miguel, said he gonna know once his lawyer got the discovery.

Aight, Alex said as he got the 5 bundles and left. I'm finna go move in his crib tonight, Manny said, what about you? He asked Alex, Naw I' ma stay here for a while, deck this mfka out, shidd move Lil Sam here with you then, you know he tryna get away from Tracy ass, Alex said as they got off the elevator and met up with Lil Sam. Aye, Lil Sam, you wanna move in with me, Alex said? Hell yea I'm tired of my OG steady bringing random niggas in the crib. I'm moving in tonight, Lil Sam jokes. Aight that's cool Alex said starting the car up. Aye, Alex Manny said, What's up famo? What you think about, my sister moving in with you? I think that would be great, Alex said, switching his tone from serious to joking. That way me and Lil Sam can turn this bitch into a full-blown bachelor pad, Alex said as they pulled up to the block right on time to open up. Let's Do it y'all, Lil Sam you on the money today and I'm doing the jabs, Manny said, as they posted up. Just like yesterday, Manny ran through 3 bundles by 2:00, the only thing different is they were putting everything up because they didn't have a connect at the time. Once they got down to at least 20 bundles total they were gonna go holla at whoever was working at the set store. By 5:00 all 5 bundles were gone. Manny wrapped up the money and put it in the armrest. The trio jumped into the car and headed to the building. Once we get to Alex's crib we can divide the money up still, because we can take off what Miguel was paying and leave the rest as the re-up.

I know Miguel was getting his curve outta that shit too, so we probably got more than what we were taking off. But we can wait till we go and re-up to do all that, Manny said as they got to the building. Manny grabbed the money out of the armrest and got out. The trio walked into the building, got on the elevator, and went to Alex's crib. Damn what's that smell? Alex said entering the crib. It smells like chicken, Manny said as Alexandria emerged from the kitchen. Smell good huh, she said. When the fuck you learn how to cook like that, Lil Sam said. Boy, I'm grown as hell, Alexandria said, walking up to the stove. Manny sat down and pulled out all the money from the block. Manny counted the money up it totaled $12,500, he put $7,500 up and divided the $5,000 between the 3 of them from 2 days they had $16,500, put up, and 6 bundles left. Can you drive Alexandria? Manny asked her, yea, I'm a senior, I did take driver's ed she said, ok cool, let me holla at you real quick, Manny said, walking to her bedroom. Wassup boo she said? You wanna move in with me? Manny said, boy, you live down the hall from me, fuck I' ma live with you. Man look here I' ma ask you one more time, Do you wanna move in with me? Yea, aight grab what you need and let's go, Manny said, and don't bring any of that old shit, I' ma give you some money to go shopping when you get outta school tomorrow. Alright, she said getting the shit that she just brought with the money Alex just gave her.

Aye, I'm bout to ride out, but I'll be over here early in the morning, after we knock them last 6 bundles off we gonna holla at them people at the set store, Manny said as he and Alexandria left out the crib.

Chapter 7

Boy! Where are you taking me? Alexandria said as she got off on Sheridan. We are going to my crib, I told you, Manny said. Pullover in front of that building to your right. Come on, Manny said as she parked the car. Manny grabbed her bag and they walked into the building when they entered, Manny nodded at the lady at the front desk and jumped on the elevator. Push 23 he told Alexandria. Whose house is this she said? Why are you asking so many questions? Come on, they walked to 3c, and Manny search through the keys to finding the correct one, after finding the right key and opened the door, Alexandria damn near fainted. The plush apartment looked like heaven to her, being that all she knew was the dirty projects. Damn, this you for real, ours Manny corrected her.

My homie gave me the crib, the rent paid up for the year, so get comfortable, Manny said as Alexandria went to the window looking at the lakefront. Ohh this shit making me horny, I'm finna go shower, she said. Manny went into the bedroom and removed all of Miguel's shit from the drawer and closet, placing it into the closet in the hallway, so he could make room for him and Alexandria's shit. Once everything was moved he searched for the bag that the work was in. He found what he was looking for on the shelf in the back of the closet. Manny grabbed the bag, opened it up, and poured it out on the bed, it was at least a brick. Half already packaged up, ready to be sold. Aw yea it's lit, Manny said to himself. Tossing the bag back into the closet. Manny took his shoes and shirt off and sat on the couch, turned the TV on, and put the sports center on. My Bday is less than 30 days, I turn 17, I gotta do it big, he said to himself. I gotta get it in tho, then find a new connect, I hope this nigga Miguel call before this shit all gone, Manny thought to himself.

The bathroom door opened up and Alexandria stepped out looking like JuJu from Love and Hip-Hop. She was oiled up so her caramel skin was glowing, Her curly hair was in a ponytail, her breast sat up like she had just got her tities done. Her pussy was neatly shaved and that ass was plump. For her to be 17, she had a body like a 25-year-old woman. She walked up to Manny and straddled him, what took you so long to say something to me, she said? I was waiting to get my money right so I could get us outta them projects, Manny replied. That is not an excuse, you supposed to have got up with me, she said, you better be glad I ain't go nowhere else. You know you belong to me. Manny said, turning her over onto the couch, and kissing her passionately. Alexandria pulled Manny's shorts and boxers off, pushing him off of her. What? Manny said confused, come here, she said as she grabbed Manny's dick when he got near. She placed it in between her lips and sucked like it was a bomb pop. She had Manny going crazy, she knew it too. She was Manny's first, so she planned on putting her stamp on him. She was gagging and coughing as she deep throated Manny's dick. Alexandria was a virgin too, besides being raped constantly by Claude, Manny was her first. Claude gave her all the experience tho. Aw, shit baby 'i'm about to cum, Manny said, tapping her shoulder but Alexandria kept sucking until she felt Manny's load coming, she pulled his dick out of her mouth right when he was cumming and shot it all over her face and mouth. She smeared it all over her mouth with his dick. Damn Manny said, dropping down to the couch still hard, aw you still hard, Alexandria said, with nut all over her face, she got up and straddled Manny, inserting his dick in her pussy, and started riding him like a cowgirl. I want you to fuck me in the window, she said. Manny picked her up and carried her over to the window, placing her back against the glass. Manny pounded her pussy like he was fresh outta jail. I'm cumming bae, Alexandria yelled squirting all over Manny's dick. Manny started pumping even faster as he neared orgasm, I'm finna cum baby, Manny yelled, me too she said.

You gone have my baby, Manny asked her, yes baby, put a baby in me, fuck, fuck, fuck, Alexandria yelled as she came again for the second time, Manny came right behind her, shooting his load all in her. They both collapsed on the floor and didn't move for the rest of the night.

Chapter 8

The next morning, Manny was up at 6:00 am, for 2 reasons, one to get Alexandri to school and to get a jump start on opening up the corner. You ready bae, Alexandria said, getting out of the shower, yea I'm waiting on you, Manny said, then his phone started ringing. He didn't recognize the number, so he answered it and disguised his voice. Hello, Manny said. This is a collect call from Miguel, to accept the charges press 1. Manny pressed 1 immediately. What's up Lil Homie? Miguel said, shit about to head out, you already know, Manny replied. That's, what's up! Aye you been to the crib yet, Miguel, asked? Nigga, me and my lady finna leave from outta here right now. Miguel laughed, ok, ok, I see you my nigga, you got that bag, right? Miguel asked. Yep, it's on my lap right now. I'm finna go to the building and get shit situated, Manny replied, aight, bet. That should have you good for a minute, when its ova with go to the set store and holla at Big El, tell'em I sent you and tell'em what's going on with me. He is going to take care of everything else, Miguel said. Alright, you need something else, Manny said, yea Miguel replied, send yo lady up here to put $10,000 in my commissary account. Damn, if I give you that, what imma have to get up with Big El? Nigga go in the hallway closet, it's a safe in there, punch in 7414 and you do the rest of the math. Look I' ma be down for a while, I need you to be on point for me, this shit can drag out for years. You run it up and have something for me when I get home Lil nigga, Miguel said. My Lawyer will call you when I need you to do something else for me, you already know what I'm talking about, Miguel said. Aight, say less, Manny said, as the call ended.

Manny jumped up and ran to the closet in the hallway, tossing all the shit that he put in the closet yesterday onto the floor. As he moved the last shoebox, he noticed a square box in the corner with numbers on the side of it. Manny punched 7414 in and the safe popped open, stacks of bills were piled on top of each other. Manny pulled all the money and sat them on the counter, Alexandria came walking into the living room and saw all the money on the counter and shouted, damn baby, where you get all that money from. Be the fuck quiet, you wanna tell all the neighbors, Manny snapped. Count that money real quick, before we leave, Manney told her. She sat at the counter and counted every bill to the last dollar, Bae, this is $97,600, damn Manny said, under his breath. Ok, take $13,000 out of that. I need you to go down to the County and put $10,000 in Miguel Santo's account, then do what with the $3,000, Alexandria said. I know you really ain't gotta go to school today because it's the end of the school year, so take the day off and go shopping, get ya feet and nails done, go get a Brazilian wax and buy you some clothes and shit. Aw thank you, baby, she said running up and kissing Manny all over his face. Grab that bag, he told Alexandria, as they walked out the door and jumped on the elevator. I' ma go put the money in his account after I drop yall off on the block, Alexandria said. As they got off the elevator and walked to the car. 30 minutes later Manny and Alexandria were pulling up to the building. Alexandria still has her keys to the apartment, so they walked right in. Lil Sam was knocked out on the couch and Alex was sleeping in Claud's old bedroom with a box of pizza in the bed with him. Look at these 2 clowns, Manny said, tossing the cup of water that was on the table in Lil Sam's face. What the fuck? Lil Sam said as he jumped up thinking he was drowning. Nigga I text both of you clowns over an hour ago and said, I was on my way! Manny snapped. The noise woke Alex up, he came running out of the bedroom to see what was going on. Yall get ready man, I found the other work Miguel had stashed and he had some money too. I just talked to him. He said, to gone and do us, just have something for'em when he comes home. So let's get it in, Manny said, emptying the work on the table.

Damn, that's a lot of work, Lil Sam said, man, this ain't shit, we need to run through this shit. So, starting today we open until 10 pm we need everything coming. So we taking the last 6 bundles and 4 more. We need to do 10 bundles a day for now, then go up to 15, and so on. We ain't settling no more. We need to take our show on the road too. We need to go elsewhere, not just this corner, we need multiple spots, Manny said. Let's get to it, Alex replied. Alex goes to put the bag up except for the 10 bundles we are taking with us and yall get ready so we can bounce, Manny said as Lil Sam went to the washroom to get ready. Alex brushed his teeth and washed his face in the kitchen sink. Yo nasty ass, his sister said. Alex stuck his middle finger up at her. Give me a kiss baby, Manny said, puckering up his lips as Alexandria tongued him down. What do you wanna do for your bday? You know it's three weeks away, Alexandria said. I don't know yet! Manny said. We'll figure it out tho. Lil Sam came out of the washroom and Alex had just finished brushing his teeth. Yall ready? Lil Sam said. Yup

Alex said wipe the cole out of his eyes. Come on then Manny said, opening the door to leave out. Alex grabbed the 10 bundles and the Draco, coming out last. They all jumped into the G8 and smashed off. As Alexandria turned the corner on 39th, Manny sat up in the seat, who the fuck is that on our shit? He said as Alexandria pulled up to the corner. Manny let the window down, yall niggas lost or something, he asked the older 3 niggas posted up on the corner. Naw nigga, you must be lost the older guy said, Miguel is gone now, so this is free enterprise, dude said, checking Manny. Let me out, Alex said, as Manny opened his door, then Alexandria let Lil Sam out. As all three jumped out, the older cats looked at how small they were and laughed. What yall gonna do call ya uncles or something? Get the fuck outta here, Dude said. Naw we ain't going nowhere, Alex said, pulling the Draco from behind his back. Now unless Niggas wanna be getting scraped up off the fuckin ground, I suggest yall get the fuck on before I let this bitch go, Alex said, waving the gun between the 3 men. Aight,

Lil homie you got it, one of the older cats, said, as they scurried off down the block. Next time I want to be as nice, Alex yelled. Goofy ass niggas, Manny said as he looked at Alex. Yall ready to open up, Manny asked, what the fuck you think, Lil Sam said as he went across the street to post up in the cut to do lookout, as Manny gave Alexandria a kiss and hug. You be careful out here baby! She said. I am, make sure you be here at 10 to pick us up and go straight to the County to drop that money, he said, as she got back into the car and pulled off.

Fiend after fiend came up. I don't know what Miguel put on this dope but this shit is the thang! Manny said as a car pulled up. By 11:00 am they had sold 6 bundles, with 4 more left. We out here until 10 from here on out Lil Sam told the hypes. Thank God! One of the hypes walked up and said we hate when yall close shop, that shit them other niggas got ain't shit like yalls. We got yall auntie, Manny said. Alex, we need 10 more bundles, we damn near done Lil Sam yelled across the street. Aight, nigga call yo bitch and tell her to grab 'em, she know where they at, Alex snapped. Watch yo mouth! Manny said, as he pulled his phone out and called Alexandria. Yea bae I'm here right now, she said answering the phone. Aye, as soon as you are done at the County, I need you to swing back around to yall crib and grab me 10 more of those, Manny said. Aight, she said, sounding pissed off. Be cool bae, you gonna be able to do yo Lil spa day, Manny said, knowing that was the reason she was pouting. Alright, she said, I should be there in 30 minutes, she said, ending the call. She said 30 minutes, Manny told Lil Sam, aight bet. We should be cool till then, Lil Sam said. By noon they had run through 9 bundles and working on the last one by 1 pm. Damn today a good day, Lil Sam said, excitedly. Aint it, man, Manny said as Alexandria pulled up with the other 10 bundles, Manny grabbed them and put them in Lil Sam slot, so when he was done with the jab he was working on he would have another one to start on. By 9:00 pm Lil Sam was halfway through with the other 10 bundles. With only five bundles left, Manny had decided to shut it down for the night, yall I just texted Alexandria and told her to pull up. She said, she's 10 minutes away. Aight, Alex said. Lil Sam was serving a fiend when he saw a shadow in the gangway. Who the fuck is that? Lil Sam, yelled, where's Alex? Fucking off in the building, it could be the law, Lil Sam stepped into the gangway to see if he could see who it was, but no one was there. I'm finna go around to the alley, entering the alley, he saw that the garbage can had been moved, so he stepped back and chirped Alex, pop out Alex and come to the alley, Manny said. As soon as he said that, one of the niggas earlier popped up from behind the garbage can, didn't I tell yo bitch ass this was my corner, he said as Manny took off running. The dude was squeezing off without aiming, hitting everything but his target. Alex came from around the corner with the Draco, aiming directly at the garbage can as he blew 7 holes into it, one hole went into the dude's arm as he ran down the alley. Alex ran behind him, blowing the Draco into his direction, another bullet landed right in the center of the dude's back, as he fell to the ground. Alex was about to stand over him and finish him off until Manny called after him.

Let's go before the Law comes, Manny said, as Alex turned around, ran to the car, he heard Dude coughing and trying to crawl up the alley. Manny, Lil Sam, and Alex jumped into the car with Alexandria and went straight to Miguel's crib.

Chapter 9

Manny, Alex, and Lil Sam sat on the sectional in the front room not saying one word. Alex broke the silence by saying, I think I killed that bitch. I hope not, Manny said, that's bad for business, them niggas tried to get down on us and you over here hoping the nigga still alive, Alex snapped. Bro, that shit can shut our whole operation down, if they find a nigga dead on our shit, Manny snapped. We don't have other blocks to go on, Miguel made that shit possible, so hold it down, Manny said. On top of that, we don't even know where the niggas from or who they are. We gotta be on point at all times and we only got one gun at that, Manny added. I can help with that, Lil Sam chimed in. My cousin, he from Englewood, they call their hood Willie Ville, they got that type of shit and they like playing crazy too, Lil Sam said. I know for sure they'll come through if it involves money and we can put some shit on their block too, Lil Sam said. Aight, call'em up, Manny Said. In the meantime, I need to run through this money we moved today.

Alexandria, Manny called out, What? Who the fuck you, what, Manny replied? I'm just playing baby, she said. Count that, Manny said, tossing her the bag. She went to the room and counted the money, while Lil Sam was on the phone with his cousin. Ok, cool Lil Sam said hanging up. Cuz said he'll be at my crib in the morning with the poles and some of his goons too, so we can chop it up, Lil Sam added. Aight bet Manny said. Alexandria came back into the front room in her Lil bitty ass boy shorts, with the bottom of her ass cheeks hanging out and a tank top that her nipples were damn near tearing through. $9750, she said tossing the money on the counter, then walking off. That's decent, but if we open up at 6 am and close at 10 pm we can easily do a dub a day especially if we pump the bags up, Manny said. We should just leave it the way it is, Alex said. Naw, I'm tryna get rich, Bro, this shit ain't forever, Manny snapped. Nigga if we pump the bags up, the hypes gonna come back even more, then we expand to other blocks and start serving niggas weight. We can do damn 200,000 a day if we want to, Manny said. Now that's what I'm talking about, Lil Sam chimed in. We gotta go hard or go home, Manny said, looking at Alex. Alex shook his head in agreement. Now let's get some sleep, so we can pop out early, scope the scene out, then meet Lil sam's peoples, Manny said, going into the room. Aw yea, I'm going to the set store tomorrow to holla at Dude nem about some more work, Manny said. But we ain't got all the money yet, Lil Sam replied. Yea we do, we got the money Miguel left, we gonna use all that to get more work and stack the shit that we made already. Then when all the work we buy plus the shit we still got is gone, we take our profit off the top, then re-up again, Manny said, walking into the bedroom.

The next morning the crew was up early. They left Alexandria in the rib. So they would have the car to themselves. First, Alex rode through the block to see if anything looked outta place, then he hit the alley to see if any red tape was back there, but there wasn't any. So they pulled to the building and went upstairs to wait for Lil Sam people to come. It was 7:30, they said they would be there at 8:00 am, so they wouldn't be late opening up. Lil Sam's phone rang, yoo Lil Sam yelled into the receiver, aight the 13th floor, he said hanging up. That's them right there coming up, Lil Sam said, opening the door, so his people know what apartment they were in. Right here fool, Lil Sam yelled as his people got off the elevator. What's up Cuz? Lil Sam said to his cousin, who was first through the door, followed by 3 other niggas. Cuz, this my nigga Alex and Manny. They dapped each other up and introduced everybody else. Bowie, Lil Sam's cousin was the one with the guns, so he did all the talking. Aight homie, I got some 50 shot Glocks, 30 shot Glocks, Draco's, and some 40 cals. I bought 3 of each, for yall, I'll give y'all everything for 6 bucks, Bowie said. With no hesitation Manny said we'll take'em, tossing Bowie the rubberband of money, that's 10 bucks. We might need y'all assistance for a while if y'all don't mind, Manny said, it's gonna be beneficial for y'all too, Manny added. Shid, I already like how you move, whatever you need we got y'all, Bowie said. Aight look, Manny got straight to it. Letting them know what had happened the day before and how they were tryna expand. We got y'all, Bowie said, we've been tryna get some shit started on our end anyway he said. I see y'all got shit, so we can definitely move it. We got damn near the whole Englewood fucking with us anyway. So, we can get up with other niggas too and have them, cop, from us, I heard about how y'all shit rolling. Everybody in our hood shit is stepped on, Bowie said. So once we give them a taste of our shit, they ain't gonna have a choice but to cop. Alright, then cool, this how we gonna do it, Manny said, tossing Bowie 20 - 50 bundles bring me $9,000 off that and you keep the $4,000, pay your people or whatever you do then we can go from there. If you need more, that shit on deck. Let's take the city over, Manny said to Bowie. Bowie dapped Manny and got up. I' ma leave a couple of my best hitta's, with yall tho, While I go get this shit started, Bowie said, leaving out. The 3 hittas, Manny, Alex, and Sam grabbed the guns they needed and headed to the block to open up. 10 minutes later they were right on time to open the corner up. Alex was in his usual slot along with another hitta with him, the other 2 hittas were scattered out down the block, sitting on abandoned porches and shit, while Manny and Lil Sam sold the jabs.

What you think, Lil Sam said to Manny? It's a team effort, Manny said. I'm about to walk to the set store tho, Manny said, spinning off. Aye come walk with me, Manny said to Chuck. Manny filled Chuck in on everything that's going on around there from the police to the bitches. By the time they made it to the store, Chuck felt like he was from the block. What's going on Papi, Manny said walking up to the counter, nothing much, you know me Papi said. Hey I need to talk to you real quick, Manny said, Papi opened the door so Manny could come in the back. What's on your mind? Youngin Papi said. Miguel sent, I already know Big El stopped Manny, mid-sentence. Come see me tomorrow night, bring all the money you can, because I don't do small-time and I don't need all the traffic. I'll give you enough shit, to hold you over for a couple of months, Big El said, motioning for Manny to leave out. Alright, see you tomorrow, but what time, Manny asked, when the store closes, Big El said, Alright Manny replied and walked out. When Manny and Chuck made it back to the block, Lil Sam had some thick ass chick in his face, aight baby I'm working right now but Ima call you later tho, so we can link up, Lil Sam said and bring yo buddies with you, alright shorty said walking off, ass looking like 2 basketballs. Damn who was shorty, Manny said, some bitch that walked down the street, Lil Sam said. She straight, Manny said. What happened with fool? Sam asked, aw we good, I'll meet him tomorrow, Manny replied. How we looking on that tho, Manny said. Talking about the bundles.

Shidd I sold like 7 jabs so far, Lil Sam replied. That's Luv right there it's only 10:15, Manny said rubbing his hands together like Birdman. 3 hours later Alex was running back to the crib to grab some more bundles. It was only 1 p.m. and they had run through 3 bundles, that's 150 jabs, Alex thought as he grabbed 3 more bundles out of the slot and drove back to the block. Alex parked on the next corner and walked up to give Lil Sam the bundles, then went back in his slot.

These bundles that Manny bought from Miguel crib must've had some extra shit on it because hypes were coming outta nowhere buying whole jabs. By 9:00 Alex had made another trip to the crib to get more jabs. Lil Sam made sure to let all the hypes know that they were opening up at 6: 00 am from now on. Chuck and the other 2 hitters saw how the money was flowing through and they wanted to get involved too. By 10:00 Manny had shut the block down and everybody went back to Alex's crib. Damn, that bitch was rolling today Lil Sam said, on my mama, Alex agreed. Manny sat on the couch and looked at all the money in the bag. So what's up he said to chuck and the other 2 hittas, D-thang and Short. Shidd you know wassup nigga, we finna come down here with you and get this money, Chuck said. Manny started smiling, aight shidd we gonna take shifts then you and yo squad take a shift and we'll get a shift, then we switch every day. Then once we see how the line is doing on y'all end. We can rotate thru there too, Manny said. Everybody agreed on that and Manny got up to leave, Alex come and drop me off, he said, matter of fact, I'm good, I'll catch an uber, Manny said, pulling out his phone, 30 minutes later Manny was pulling up to the crib in his uber. Soon as he walked through the door he could smell the oils on Alexandria's body coming from the bedroom. Manny walked into the bedroom and gave her the bag for her to count the money. She laid there in a red thong and matching bra, with her hair curled. Her feet were freshly done and Manny knew what she wanted, him. When you're done I'm finna tear that pussy up, Manny said, going to the shower.

Lil Sam, Alex, Chuck, and the 2 hittas sat on the couch playing Madden until the door buzzer went off. Who the fuck is this Alex said, that's shorty nem from earlier Lil Sam smiled. She better have somebody for me, Alex said, opening the door.

Two of the prettiest bitches Lil Sam ever saw come walking in. Damn, I ain't know y'all was gone be this deep, I would've bought my other buddies, Amber, Lil Sam's chick said, it ain't too late short said, it is because they went out already, but I' ma text them to slide, if we still here when they done, Amber said. Aw yall gone be here Lil Sam said, grabbing Amber by her hand, walking to his room. What's yo name baby, Alex asked her friend, Asia she replied. Hey Asia I'm Alex, What's up Alex? Asia replied. Chuck and the other 2 hitters weren't waiting around for some mystery bitches, so they left. We'll be back at 5:30 am, Chuck said, walking out. Aight bro Alex said. So where is your man at? Alex asked, I ain't got one, Asia replied, damn a woman as fine as you, with no man, that ain't right, Alex said. I'm waiting for the right man, Asia said, well you found him, Alex smiled, Is that right she replied, yep, ok we'll see, Asia said, we will want we, Alex replied.

Chapter 10

After Alexandria had counted the money, it came out to $29,250 and that was just a day's work. That had Manny charged up. He came out with the $84,700 Miguel had stashed, the $70,000 they had mover over the time that they had been serving too, he put the $29,250 up tho so altogether he had $154,950 on him the way to the building. Lil Sam was geeked up too, he was the one that called and woke Manny up at 5:00 am. When Manny got to the building everybody was there. Chuck, Alex, Lil Sam, D-thang, and Short. Manny told Alexandria to stay at the building with the money and that when he called, bring the money down. Mann and Lil Sam agreed to let Chuck and his crew work the 1st shift so the fiends could get used to seeing them. Manny gave it to them like

Miguel, gave it to them, take 30 off each jab, its 50 jabs in a bundle, once yall do a bundle each one of yall clear 500 a piece and turn in 5 bucks. The 1st shift was from 6 to 2 and Manny, Lil Sam, and Alex would take over from 2 to 10. Alex, Manny, and Sam did security while the other crew worked. By 2:00 Chucks crew ran through 10 bundles. Giving them $5,000 each and turning in $50,000 the second shift went just as well, doing 9 bundles bringing today's total to $108,500. Manny couldn't believe his eyes as he saw all the many coming in. He pulled out his phone and told Alexandria to pull up with the bag. She was there in less than 5 minutes. I'll meet y'all at the building manny said, to Alex and the rest of the crew. Pull up to the Set Store Manny said. Alexandria pulled off and turned 2 corners and was at the Set Store. Manny remembered that Big El told him to bring all the money he had, so he put the $108,500 with the $154,950 and went into the store. Wassup Papi? Manny said as he walked behind the counter, nothing much I was about to leave your ass was taking too long, Papi said. Come on Papi said walking into the back. Papi opened a barrel full to the top with dope. How much money you bring, Papi asked. This a Lil over a quarter Mil, Manny said, tossing him the bag. Papi's eyes got big as hell, you kidding me right, Papi sad. Manny just stood there nonchalantly as Papi looked through the bag. Damn kid, Miguel never came like this, Papi said. Alright, all this is yours, Papi said. It's already shook and packaged, all you gotta do is sell it. This is 10 bricks of uncut Colombian dope Papi said. You get caught, you never snitch, you'll be well taken care of. My lawyer is the best, he's on top of Miguel's case. He'll be home in due time, as long as there's no witness, Papi said, emphasizing, "no witness". In that bag is a half-million dollars worth of precut, you owe me a quarter mil, now go ahead, Papi said, tossing Manny the bag. Manny jumped into the car with Alexandria and went straight home, bypassing the building. He couldn't risk having all this shit in the project building. Once he got home he called Lil Sam and Alex telling them to meet him at the building and to bring Bowie too. An hour later Manny, Bowie, Lil Sam, and Alex were sitting in his living room, aw, here got something for you Bowie said, tossing him the money, they love that shit my way dawg, Bowie said. I gotta few niggas that wanna cope some shit too. Aight Manny said they gotta go through you tho, but the thing is we only selling our shit in bundles. We don't give a fuck what they do with it when they buy it as long as they don't sell it on our joints and stepping on it, we good, Manny said and everybody agreed. So they gotta buy bundles Bowie asked, hell yeah that's how my man is giving it to me so the shit can stay consistent, and we don't know if it's gonna be potent enough, Manny said. I can dig it Bowie agreed.

Manny took the $10,000 Bowie had given him and put it with the rest of the money ($29,700) he had put up. Aight Bowie I' ma give you 2 bricks to get your people right, you run through that quick enough, I'll give you 5 when you come back, Bowie nodded his head. You're gonna make at least $90,000 off each one, you bring me $50,000 off

each one, cool Manny asked and Bowie said Hell,
yeah we cool. I have been needing some shit like this
for a minute. Aight then hit the line in the A.M. and
I got Chuck, Dthang, and Short, so you get the rest
of ya guys together with that, Manny said. We need
to get some more blocks, Manny told Bowie. I got
that on lock already. I' ma have my people on every
block in Englewood by the weekend, Bowie said
walking out. So we got $40,000 put up right now,
I'm finna divide that up between us 3 that's like
$13,000 a piece, I' ma give Alexander that odd G
for all she does, Manny said. Now Papi is giving us
the bricks for $25,000, I'm charging Bowie $50,000
which is fair because he's still doubling his money
anyway. That extra $25,000 we chop down the
middle and take the other $25,000 to the store,
Manny said. Another thing, you niggas need to
move out them projects too, we finna be getting too
much money to be in these apartments. I' ma holla
at Papi and see if he can get us a realtor so we can
get sum cribs, you know we can't legally put shit in
our names because we are too young. We ain't doing

that shit anyway, Alex said, we ain't got no jobs, right Lil Sam replied. I'm sure Papi can help us out, I' ma holla at him tomorrow, Manny said. We still gonna keep the cribs we have as traps tho, but we ain't laying our heads there tho. Y'all take these 5 bricks with y'all and I' ma hold these other 18 here. We got the 1st shift tomorrow, so we out early, Manny said. After these 5 bricks are gone we're gonna let Chuck nem run that muthafucka and we just sit back and collect, Manny said. Aight bet Alex said as they walked out.

Chapter 11
A Month Later

After 1 week, Manny, Alex, and Lil Sam weren't even serving anymore. Chuck and his crew were on the corner doing 5 bundles a day. That's $39,500 and $276,500 a week. They paid the crew $45,000 a week, that's $15,000 a piece. Manny and nem were bringing in $8,295,000 a month off the corner alone. Bowie had the whole Englewood on lock if you weren't copping from him, you couldn't serve. He had a hit team in place for whoever wanted smoke and they were thirsty to nail something. Bowie was bringing in every bit of $50-$60K a day just off the block, not including the shit he had going on, on other blocks. Papi had sat Manny up with a real estate agent that he fucked with. She had everything put together as long as you had the money. Paperwork wasn't a problem, she had names, socials, and everything as long as that bag was right, you were good. I' ma holla at yall later, I'm gonna go check this spot out, Manny said, hopping in the car with Alexandria. They rode to a secluded area out in Richton Park. The agent was in the driveway waiting when they pulled up. Hi, I'm Alicia, she said, I'm Manny and this is my girl Alexandria, Manny said, shaking Alicia's hand.

You look quite young Alicia said, sizing Manny up. What that supposed to mean Alexandria said. Aw, nothing I didn't mean anything by it Alicia checked herself. Um huh, Alexandria said as they went into the crib. As you can see, we'll take it, Manny said, cutting Alicia off. Aw ok, then this house will cost you $249,000 that with my fee included Alici said. Manny nodded at his lady and she tossed Alicia the bag. That's a quarter Mill, but I want it in her name, make it make sense, Manny said to Alicia. I'm not buying a crib for all this paper and it's in somebody else's name, Manny said, my girl is going to college next month and she turns 18 in a few weeks so make it look good, Manny said. I got you since Big El referred you, Alicia said. I'll meet you in a few days with all the paperwork and the keys, Alicia said. I got appointments with a few of your other homies too, Alicia said. I know get'em right, Manny said as he and Alexandria left out. When they got back in the care Alexandria couldn't stop smiling. I love you, baby, she said, I love you too, Manny replied. Now let's get the fuck outta here, Manny said. Alexandria drove off going back to the hood. I'm buying you a new car tomorrow too, he said, you are, Alexandria perked up. Yea I have been looking at that new BMW Truck that X7, Manny said. You'll look good in that, we gotta get outta this, I' ma trap outta this bitch. I can almost drive. I just can't park yet, Manny said, we'll just have to work on parking then Alexandria said as she pulled up to the corner. So what club we are going to tomorrow for your birthday, she said. I don't know probably Club O. I'll let you know when I make it home. Ima stop by my O.G. crib and give her some bread it's up to her what she does with it, Manny said. As he got out of the car, what happened, Alex said? Shit, the crib was so fucking big and nice. I had to cash out on that bitch, Manny said, aw hell yea, I suppose to meet up with her Monday Lil Sam said, mine Tuesday Alex chimed in. It's lit then, Manny said, naw it's lit tomorrow for yo Muthafuckin bday, Alex said. Yea I'm thinking Club O, Manny said. Hell yea I like their bitches, Chuck said from across the street ear hustling. We're there then, Manny said. I gotta go find something to wear tho in the morning, Manny said, nigga we all do, Alex said. Aight we gone slide downtown in the morning, Manny said. I'm finna pimp to the building real quick and holla at my O.G. Manny said. I'll walk with you, Lil Sam replied, I need a break my O.G. off real quick. It took about 10 minutes for them to get to the building. Chirp me when you are done, Manny said to Lil Sam as he entered the apartment. Ma, Ma, Manny yelled. He got no response but he heard a smacking noise, so he walked into the room and saw his mama on her knees sucking some fat black nigga dick like her life depended on it.

Manny just turned around and walked out, it's useless he thought she would never change.

All the money in the world couldn't help her, she was too far gone. Manny was glad he was the only child, he chirped Lil Sam, I'm in the front of the building when you are done, Manny said. I'm coming down, her stupid ass ain't even her Lil Sam said. The 2 met up in front of the building and walked back to the block talking about how fucked up their O.G's were.

Chapter 12

The next morning, they were 4 cars deep on their way downtown to Barney's to get their shit together for the party. Manny had given Alexandria $5,000 to buy her something nice to wear, Lil Sam did the same with Amber and Alex with Asia. Amber and Asia were actually in their car trailing Alex and Lil Sam so they could see what they were wearing, trying to match their niggas. All cars pulled up simultaneously in from of Barney's door with all the occupants hopping out, not giving a fuck about any tickets. Manny bought a Balmain Mannequin with some red bottoms too. Alex grabbed a DSquared fit with some Gucci shoes. Chuck and everybody else was all around the store grabbing all types of shit. Asia copied exactly what Alex grabbed but the women's addition and Amber brought a Balenciaga shirt, with some Balenciaga shoes and a pair of leather Vera Wang Capris. Altogether they spent at least $50,000 in Barneys. As they left, Manny was feeling like he needed to treat himself so they pulled up to Treasures on Roosevelt, the whole squad belt out, and went in. Security was nervous as hell, steady clutching his heat. Man you good, we're here to spend money, Manny said, reaching into his Louis Vuitton man bag pulling out knots of money. How can I help you the young Arab said. How much for this P Sky-Dweller, Manny said, the bust down one is $86,000 the young Arab said. Not knowing who he was talking to. "I got $70,000 right now," Manny said, dropping the money on the center The young Arab couldn't speak, his boss had to come out and take the order, I can't do 70K Sir this is a $100,000 watch. You can do $70,000 if we all buy something, Alex said pointing to the Audemar, telling him what he wants, followed by Lil Sam telling him to give him the Patek Philippe. Hold on, the salesman said. The Audemar is 60K and the Patek Philippe is 80k, aight well give you $180,000 for all watches right now, Alex said, take it or leave it. The salesman would've been a fool to let all that money walk out of the store like that. He gave them the watches for $175,000 after Manny got through talking. They all left the store and headed to the block, tryna recoup some of that bread they just spent. When they got to the block, Short and D-Thang had the block jamming, They didn't go with Manny and the rest of the squad because somebody had to run the block while they were gone, but once everybody got back Lil Sam and Alex had Amber and Asia take D-Thang and Short to shop from head-to-head. Chuck took over the duties while Short and D-Thang were gone, Alex kept his gun on him so he was on the lookout. Manny said fuck it for old-time sake and collected the money while Chuck served fiend after fiend. 3 hours and 20 bundles later Short and D-THang were back in their slots getting to the money. I'm finna get outta here Manny said., we gonna meet up at the building at midnight so we can shoot out, Manny said as he got in the Uber and headed home.

Chapter 13

At 12:00 am, 20 cars were lined up outside of the building, on their way to the party. Who the fuck are all these people? Alex asked Bowie, these some of my people, they bought some people with them too, you know how that shit goes Bowie said dapping Alex. This everybody Manny said walking up to Bowie and Alex? Yup Bowie said. Yo man on point at the door right Manny, Asked Bowie? Nigga, what I tell you? We are good! Let's ride Bowie replied as everybody started to get in their cars and head to the club. 20 minutes later they were pulling into the parking lot. Some had to pay $40 and some $20 depending on where they parked at. After everybody got situated with their parking space they headed to the club. Like always the line was off the chain. Man, what the fuck, Manny said as he stood in the line that wrapped around the club. Bowie, what's up? Manny said, hold on, Bowie replied, cutting thru the line tryna get to the door to catch his man. About 5 minutes had passed when Manny saw Bowie and some big Suge Knight-looking mfka cutting thru the line coming directly towards them. These all my people's Bowie told the bouncer. Aw yeah, this gonna cost you the bouncer added.

Bowie went into his man backpack and pulled out 50 blue strips handing them to Suge Knight. Aw ok, then he said fanning the money. All y'all come with me, Suge said, as the entourage followed behind the bouncer, knocking niggas over and stepping on niggas shoes. Alex bumped into this one female, knocking her purse off her arm, damn my bad baby, Alex said tryna pick the purse up, outta nowhere some nigga jumped in talking hella shit, already mad he had to stand in line, then Alex knocked his bitch bag on the ground add fuel to the flame. Bitch ass nigga you betta watch where you going the dude said. Alex spits in the nigga face, who the bitch now, Alex said, the nigga tried to bust on Alex, but Lil Sam was already in arms reach and gave the nigga a one hitta quitta, ending his night for sure, Alex and the rest of the crew then headed into the club. Once they entered the club Manny, Alex, and Lil Sam were looking around, like they were outta town. The scene looked like some shit in a movie, the trio had never been in the club before, so this was all new to them. It was bitches sliding down poles, dancing naked, and serving bottles. We over here Bowie said, breaking Manny out of his trance. They all walked into the section that seemed a block long. Damn, this bitch crack-in, Chuck said. I swear it is, Manny agreed. As they took a seat, the bottle girl came and asked what kind of bottles they wanted. Uh, Don Julio, Aevejo, Dusse, Remy 1738, Patron, and Jose Moet, Manny said, Ok how many of each she replied. 10 of each, Manny said. Alright, the bottle girl said spinning off. Aw, bring us 20,000 singles too, Manny added. She turned around with a huge grin on her face, going to place the order. She wasn't a stripper but for that money, she might've become one tonight. Alexandria was sitting on Manny's lap letting every bitch know who her man was. You good baby Manny asked her, of course why you say that she replied. No reason, just checking on you Manny said, placing wet kisses on her lips. Sweet ass nigga, Alex said joking, how he sweet Asia said, he just loves his bitch, goofy. I love my bitch too, Alex said, grabbing Asia's ass and holding her tight. Aw shit, it's on now the bottles are here, Lil Sam said as the bottles girls came with bottles after bottles into the section. Alex grabbed a Remy bottle, Manny followed suit with a bottle of Moet. The whole section was turned up, muthafuckas that weren't even with the crew, starting coming into the section when every stripper in the club invaded the section. They had it like 99 freak nick in that bitch, it was 3 bitches to every nigga. It was so much smoke in the air that you could barely see.

Manny and Alexandria had 3 strippers by them, catching every dollar they threw. Manny whispered in Alexandria's ear to go get the car and pull it around when they got ready to leave. She said ok and they finished partying. By the time the bottles and money were all gone, it was damn near 5 am. Manny tapped one of the hittas to walk his girl out to the car, as they were all prepared to go. Alex and Lil Sam sent their bitches too. Manny knew that the block still had to be opened at 6:00 am so he motioned to Chuck to check it out. What's up, Bro? Chuck said you know we gotta open up in an hour, Manny said. Nigga I'm 10 steps ahead of you, my Lil man'nem already on top of that, we good, Big Dawg, you ain't gotta worry about that type of shit no more, you just keep us flooded with the shit and we'll handle the rest, Chuck said, that's why I love you, Manny said, sounding like Rico from Paid in Full. Let's ride tho, Alex walked up and said. The crew gathered everybody and headed out the section walking towards the door. They were damn near the last people in the club, when they left, wasn't shit but empty bottles and bouncers in the club as they got to the exit. When they got outside it was damn near daylight. Damn Lil Sam said as he walked up to his car. Everybody who didn't have their ladies bring their car to the door was heading in different directions, hitting their alarms. Out of nowhere an all-black Charger, tinted out appeared at the front end of the lot, nobody saw it, but Chuck. The car was speeding in their direction, then the passenger side windows come down and 2 light-skinned niggas jump out, the one that Alex spit on and another nigga starting letting shots fly in the direction of Alex and Lil Sams's car and whoever was in the way. Chuck started blowing back and so did every other hitta after he took cover. Lil Sam's car was riddled with bullets and so was Manny's because when the shots went off Alexandria tried to pull up to block the bullets from hitting her brother. The gunmen emptied their clips and scratched out the lot, everybody ran to the cars that had been hit. As Lil Sam raised up in his seat he saw that Amber had been shot in the stomach and the chest. He instantly pulled her out of the car and into Manny's car, we gotta go, Lil Sam said, she's hit, he yelled, but what he didn't know was that Alexandria was hit too, in her shoulder along with Manny with wounds in his arm, leg and a graze wound in his head. Aye, Aye, Lil Sam yelled as everybody came to Manny's car pulling them out.

We gotta get them to the nearest hospital, Alex said as they pulled Amber out of the car and put her in the car with Alex. Bowie put Manny and Alexandria in his car with him. We finna go to Christ, y'all take the cars to the hood and meet us at the hospital, Bowie said as they left the scene, headed to Christ Hospital.

Chapter 14

The entire gang was in the ER waiting for updates for Manny, Alexandria, and Amber. Them niggas dead, Alex yelled in tears. She tried to save me, them, bullets were meant for me, Alex said. We gonna find them niggas, Bowie said. Imma have my homie get the surveillance tapes so we can track the car down. This shit is far from over, Bowie added. Anyone here for Alexandria Pope, the doctor said, yes me I'm her brother, Alex said, how is she, she's doing fine the doctor said. She lost a lot of blood tho, if you didn't get her here when you did, she might not have made it, the doctor said. Can I see her, Alex asked, sure she's heavily sedated though, so she might be in and out. Come with me, the Doctor said. Another nurse came out, asking if anyone was there for Amber

Kirkwood and Lil Sam sprung to his feet. Yea, yea I am, Lil Sam said. Please tell me she's good, we had to do 2 surgeries, to remove the bullet out of her chest, the nurse said, one of her lungs collapsed and her arm is broken, but she'll make it, none of her injuries is life-threatening. She's in a medically induced coma right now, so you can't see her until tomorrow when she wakes, but she's fine Sir the nurse said walking off. Thank you Lil Sam said to the nurse's back as she disappeared through the white door. Man, what's up with bro Chuck said? They ass tweaking he added, about an hour went past until the doctor came and updated the gang on Manny. I assume you all are here for the 3 gunshot victims the doctor said, what the fuck you mean you assume? Asia snapped, no Ma'am I just saw all the other doctors talking to you about the other 2 victims that came in that's all. Man what's up with our homie, Chuck jumped in saying. Well Sir he's in stable condition, the bullets went straight through. We're bandaging him up now. He wants to see Alex. Alex was in the room with his sister,

Chuck said. Alright then, only 3 of you can go back, the Doctor said, as Bowie, Chuck, and Lil Sam walked to the room. Manny was sitting on the edge of the bed ready to walk out when they walked in. Y'all found anything out yet, Manny asked them. Not yet, but as soon as we leave here, I'm getting up with my man from the club to get the surveillance tape, Bowie said. You need to go get on top of that now, Manny said, we gotta take care of that shit immediately, we can't let no nigga think shit sweet. We're getting too much money out here to be letting shit like this happen, that's bad for business, Manny snapped. I'm finna go check that out now, Bowie said, leaving the room. How are Alexandria and Amber? Manny asked Lil Sam. They good Lil Sam replied. Help me up, Manny told Lil Sam stretching out his arm. Manny grabbed the crutch off the wall and strutted down to his lady room. Sir, you can't be on your feet right now the doctor said rushing in. Man watch out, Manny said heading to Alexandria's room. When he got there he saw that Alex was sitting in the chair talking to her. Hey Bae,

Manny said, walking into the room. How are you feeling? He asked her. I'm ok, better know that I know yall good she said. The doctor said I'll be released tomorrow, so make sure yall here to get me she said. Yo get you some rest tho, Manny said, nodding his head at Alex to check it out. We'll be here 1st thing in the morning, Manny said as they left out the room. I need you to swing by the slot up north and grab that bag of money in the closet, I need to get with Big El for the re-up, Manny told Alex. Aight I'm finna go over there now Alex said, tapping one of the hitters as they left the hospital. Manny went back to his room and got dressed, even though he wasn't discharged yet he still had planned on leaving. After he had his shit on him and Chuck got on the elevator with the entire ER with them. Manny had one thing on his mind and that was murder.

Chapter 15

When Manny and the rest of the guys arrived at the projects, all eyes were on them. Everybody had heard about the incident and was trying to see how they reacted. Manny, Lil Sam, and Chuck went upstairs to the trap to wait on Alex with the money for the re-up. That was them pussy ass niggas that you knocked out, Manny said to Lil Sam. I know, Lil Sam replied. Once Bowie gets the tape, we can have Asia runs the plates and gets a location, you know her O.G. the Law, Lil Sam said. Um huh, Chuck agreed. You got Shawty nem on point on the corner, Manny asked Chuck, yup and I had some extra hitta's pop out too so if a nigga play crazy today it's gone be a massacre. What about in Englewood tho? You already know it's like Baghdad around there already. Bowie get them niggas on top of buildings with AR's and all types of shit Chuck reiterated. Aight then, so we just gotta locate these niggas and smash 'em, Lil Sam, chimed in. In mid-conversation Alex came walking in with the bag of money, tossing it on the couch. Aight, I'm finna go meet Papi. I need all y'all with me, just in case, manny said, sitting up. Let's roll then, Alex said leading the way. The same spot, Chuck said, as they got on the elevator, Now he wants me to come to Oak Lawn some muthafucking where, Manny said as they got off the elevator and headed to their cars.

30 minutes later, Manny was entering a small Bodega on 93rd Cicero along with Lil Sam and Alex. Chuck stayed in the front looking out. What's going on? Big El said. Same shit different day, Manny replied. I heard about your Lil problem, Big El said. That ain't nothing I can't handle, Manny said. Problems are not good for business Manny, Big El stressed. I understand Papi I do, but I got it under control. I see you do Big El motion for his man to bring the bag, which was filled with 100

bricks already package and stamped as Manny liked. I like you, Manny, you're a good earner and smart too, so I' ma do you a favor, Big El said sliding a piece of paper across the table, take care of your business so we can continue ours, Big El said, getting up from the table. Manny left the bag of money on the table for Big El and gave Lil Sam the work. The trio left out the bodega and got into 2 separate cars, one with the dope and the trail care. Manny opened the piece of paper and there were two addresses on it. Manny knew that those were the addresses of the shooters.

Manny, Bowie, Alex, Lil Sam, and Chuck at Miguel's apartment with 100 bricks on the table, tryna come up with a plan on how to execute this killing. 1st thing 1st, Manny said, Bowie, you think you can handle 20 of these thangs, he said referring to the work. I can handle anything you throw my way, Bowie said. Aight then, you take 20. Chuck, we already know that block doing every bit of 7 bricks a week so you take 10 to the building with you and I' ma hold 20 more here for you, Manny said. The other 50 are for y'all Manny pointed to Alex and Slim. Now that that's out the way we need to have 2- 4 Man teams at each location, this gotta be an overkill, Manny stressed. I don't care who gets it. As long as it ain't no kids, kill'em, Manny said.

8:00 am The Next Day

Alex, chuck, short, and D-Thang was in one car at one location and Bowie had 7 of his other hittas in the front and back of the other location. Man, I can't wait till one of these niggas pop out so I can empty the clip in one of their ass, Alex said. Alex didn't even have to go, he was a made man now, he had shooters for that. But the rush from putting in work just made him feel good. Who is that? D-Thang said raising in the front seat, Where? Alex said, nigga coming outta the gain-way across the street, D-Thang said. Aw, I see him Alex said putting one up top in the Glock 19. I think that's him, Short said. It definitely looks like him, Alex said. The nigga came out of the gain-way and hit the automatic start on the charger as he stood in front of the crib. Aw yeah, that's him, Alex said finna open the door. Naw wait, Chuck said, let'em get in the car first, then we gonna block'em off and bell out. Do his ass all wrong, Chuck added. Right as they said it, the nigga started walking towards the car, hitting the locks to get in he walked around to the driver's side and opened the door hoping in. Short pulled out the parking spot flying up on the Charger, cutting it off. Chuck was the first one to get out, letting 3 bullets go through the passenger window Hittin Dude in the neck with the first bullet, the other 2 hit him in the chest. Alex came running around the car emptying his clip into the nigga face and chest, Chuck joined the party emptying the rest of his clip into the nigga also. Chuck and Alex ran back to the car, as Short scratched off leaving the scene. That was the bitch ass nigga that was shouting out the back window too, Alex said. It looks like we got company, Short said as he turned the corner from 89th and Muskegon heading to South Chicago. The Law was in a ford truck flying behind the Durango. Do your thang Short, Chuck said. Short was the getaway driver on several hits. Getting away was never a problem. Short turned off 89th street going towards 87th, he mashed on the gas bringing the truck to life sending dirt flying everywhere. In 20 seconds the truck was on 75th, leaving the police on 83rd. Short then turned down 75th and hopped on the Dan Ryan giving the truck all gas until they got to 43rd. Pull-on Forestville, my Lil bitch crib right there, D-thang said, we can park in her garage. Short did as D-thang said. Hit the alley, the garage already open, Short flew down the alley, pulled in the garage. Put the guns in the slot and they all hopped out. That was close, Alex said as they followed D-thang into the crib, Wasn't it, Chuck said in agreement.

Chapter 16

Aight, bet I'm in the building, Manny said, hanging up the phone. That was Alex nem. They said they were on a high-speed chase with the Law. They good tho Lil Sam asked? Yea, they are on the way up here now, Manny said. They say they scored, so one down two more to go, Manny said. I thought it was only 2 shooters, Lil Sam said. It was a driver, everybody gotta die, Manny said. Aw yea fa'sho, Lil sam agreed. Ten minutes later Alex and the rest of the crew come walking in. Yall straight Manny said? Of course, but my young boy right here, Alex said referring to Chuck. He gets wild! I got all the respect in the world for you homie, he was the first Nigga out of the car, put one up top and 2 in the chest. You know I had to do the overkill tho, Alex bragged, put the whole 30 clip in him you know how I do. Aight then, let's get the other ones and get back to our daily routine Manny said. Bowie nem sitting on the other location still, I'm quite sure once the news breaks about ole' boy they're gonna come out that muthafuka, Lil Sam said. Hell yea, Short agreed.

Man, I'm tired of sitting in this muthafucking car, Lil Jimmy said. These Niggas ain't coming out, It's 8:30 at night we have been out here since 8 am. Be cool nigga, Lil Watts said. 30 mo minutes we gone anyway. Right, when they were getting restless, the house they were watching lights went out and 3 Niggas came walking out. The first one was on point tho looking up and down the street and into any car that rode past. He must have the pole Lil Jimmy said, turn the knob on the light switch, so when we pop out the interior light doesn't come on. Lil Jimmy said, as he opened the door, duck down, and crept along side the cars, Lil Watts followed suit and trailed Lil Jimmy as the first Nigga walked into the street. Lil Watts ducked behind the car that dude was across from and when the dude turned his head, Lil Watts lined'em up hitting him in the back of his head, blowing his shit all over the hood of the car he was in front of. The other two Niggas started blowing back hitting nothing but cars running towards the back yard as soon as they hit the alley Lil Shuge was waiting with two baretta's filling both of 'em up with more holes than a Yeezy shirt, leaving them in the lot gasping for there last breathes.

Chapter 17

The whole gang was at Lil Sam's crib for his house warming and Amber's welcome home party. I wanna thank all y'all for coming out and bringing the gifts, Amber said holding her oxygen machine. She had to be on an oxygen machine for a month or two because of her collapsed lung. But everything else was good. Aye for real tho, I love all you niggas, especially my niggas Manny and Alex. Yall know we came from nothing together for real, we like brothers. Then my Willieville family. Bowie you my blood cousin, you already know what you mean to me nigga. Don't start crying bitch Bowie yelled out. Sending the room into laughter. Naw tho, all you nigga's done grew on me for real tho. I love yall, on top of that, we teenagers living like grown-ass men. We got beautiful women and plenty of money. The world is ours Lil Sam boasted. Aight nigga you drunk Manny said. Baby, I got a surprise for you too, Manny said pulling out the key to the X7 truck. I bought it, but with all the shit that happened I never went and got it, but it's in the driveway at home. Ain't that right Manny said nodding at Asia who was walking in with the spare key, smiling. Aw, thank you baby Alexandria said. I got a surprise for you too she said, going in her Birkin Bag pulling out a positive pregnancy test. You for real, Manny said, scooping her up off her feet and spinning around. She having my baby y'all! Manny yelled as everybody started clapping we appreciate it y'all! But let's get it in and don't forget we gotta continue to stay off the radar. We can't be having no beef shit going on that shit gone slow up the money and we need that money, Manny said laughing. Fasho Bowie said, aye check it out Bowie said to Manny. My man just came and grabbed the last of what I had. So I need another load. Aight I'm finna make it happen for you, Manny said, walking off. Hold on nigga Bowie said handing him the Tom Ford Bag filled with blue stripes. Baby, Manny said to his lady, yea bae she said. I need you to go to the building and grab

20 of those things and bring'em back here for me ok. I got you, babe, Alexandria said. Leaving the party. Manny signaled for Lil Sam to check it out.

Sam walked up and Manny told him to put the money up for him till he left. Lil Sam took the bag and spent off. The party was a success, everybody was enjoying themselves, talking shit, and getting fucked up. By the time they looked up, 2 hours had passed and Alexandria hadn't come back yet. Manny looked at his rollie and saw the time and got confused. It only takes 45 minutes to get to the slot up north from Lil Sam's crib. Manny dialed her number, but she ain't pickup. He dialed it again, no answer, something wrong, Manny said, he tapped Alex on the shoulder and motioned for him to check it out. So they went to the front of the crib. I sent ya sister to grab some work from the crib for me now she ain't answering and that was over three hours ago. Fuck Alex said, she not answering Bro, she might've got pulled over, right when they were starting to think the worst she was pulling up in the front. There she goes right there, Manny said as Alexandria walked up with the bag. Why weren't you answering, Manny said? My phone died and you know how LakeShore is on a weekday at rush hour nigga she snapped walking in. Aw yea my fault baby, Manny said right behind here I ain't never having her do that shit again,

Manny said to himself.

Chapter 18

6 Months Later

You've got a collect call from Miguel, to accept these charges press 1, Manny pressed 1 Yoo, Miguel yelled through the phone, what's up my nigga, Manny said?

Nigga you up! I ain't been hearing shit but good things about you, Miguel said. I'm not on shit Manny tried not to brag. Aye tho, my lawyer got my discovery yesterday, Miguel said, aw ok so what it's looking like, Manny asked? You already know wassup Miguel said letting Manny know in code that he needed him to get to the witness. Say no more, Manny said. Aye, go holla at Papi when you get a chance, Miguel said as they ended the call. Manny knew that Miguel wanted him to go see Papi to get the identity of the witness. The lawyer Miguel had was retained by Papi so he already knew that Papi had the info. Manny immediately dialed Alex's number. Alex answered on the first ring. What's up blood? He said into the receiver. Shit, I need to holla at ya, where are you at? Manny asked me and chuck turning corners in the hood, finna pull up on Laflin and holla at Bowie, Alex said. Aight, stay right there I'm hop in an uber and come over there, Manny said, hanging up. Manny ordered his uber, sat back, and chilled, waiting for his ride to pull up. Five minutes later his ride was outside. As Manny rode in the back of the uber, he wondered who the witness was and hoped it wasn't an old person or sum Lil kid. Sir, the driver said, calling Manny, he was so caught up in thoughts that he didn't even see the driver had pulled up on the block. My bad homie, daydreaming, Manny said, exiting the car. What's craken homie? Bowie said as Manny walked up and sat on the porch next to Chuck. Shit, my boy called last night. He finna start his trial in a minute and he needs a muthafucka to get up with the witness for him, Manny said. Get up with him like what? Bowie said, paying him off or dropping his ass. Droppin em, Manny said, Aight who is the witness? Bowie said like killing a muthafucka wasn't shit. I gotta slide on Papi and get the info, Manny said. Papi, Chuck chimed in, what he got to do with it? It's his lawyer who repin my man, Manny said. The Lawyer gave Papi a copy of the witness identity, Manny replied. Aw ok, Chuck said, So who is your man? Chuck asked another question, my man is responsible for all this paper we are getting. That's a good enough answer, Manny asked? Hell yea, Chuck said, get the info I'm on top of it Chuck added. Aight, let's pull up to the bodega in Oaklawn. Papi right there until midnight tonight, Manny said, walking up to Alex's car.

Manny, Alex, Chuck and Bowie rode to the Bodega as Money Bagg, Yo blast thru the speakers. Ten minutes later they were pulling into the Bodega lot. Yall stay in the car. I'll be right back, Manny said as he got out and walked into the Bodega, Manny walked up to the bar and asked the bartender for a shot of 1738 Remy. The bartender already knew who Manny was, so he hit the buzzer under the table to let Papi know that company was there. He gave Manny his shot and Manny killed it with one gulp. Hit me again Manny said, as Papi came out the back with a manila envelope in his hand. Manny, my friend, how are you? Papi said, making small talk. I'm good Manny replied as Papa sat next to him on the stool. That for me, Manny said nodding at the envelope. Yes, Sir, Papi said, sliding the envelope to Manny. Manny took the shot the bartender had just given him and killed it as he got up. Destroy that when you're done, Big El said, as Manny left out. That was quick, Alex said as Manny got back into the car. It doesn't take that long to get an envelope, Manny said, sliding the picture out of the envelope. When Manny looked at the pictures, he squinted his eyes because the nigga looked familiar. Why you looking like that, Chuck said, you know the nigga or sum. Naw, but I definitely saw the nigga before, Manny said, as they turned down Southwest Highway on 83rd. Aww, Manny shouted, what? everybody in the car replied.

This nigga was at my O.G. crib when me and Lil Sam walked to the building. I was finna give my O.G. some bread, but when I walked in her room, I saw her on her knees sucking this nigga dick, Manny yelled. Aw ok, so we got two reasons to kill the nigga then, Chuck said, Naw I don't give a fuck about him getting some top from my O.G., but he gotta go for getting big homie knocked, that's fasho Manny snapped. Aight, you think he at ya mom's crib now Chuck asked, I don't know but we finna check it out tho. If not, we just put the word out that we finna do a passout, I bet every fiend comes out for that, Manny said. Hell yea Alex replied as they pulled back on Laflin. Shid let me know wassup Bowie said getting out. I gotta go swerve real quick, Just hit my line he said, closing the door. Alex pulled off and headed to the projects to check on the target.

Chapter 19

2 0 minutes later, Alex was in front of the building, want me to go up with you, Alex said. Naw I'm good, Manny said as he got out and walked into the building. As Manny entered the building, he stood in front of the elevator waiting on the door to open. When the door opened Manny thought it was Christmas, his heart damn near skipped a beat when he saw the mark getting off the elevator. Aye homie, check it out Manny said. What's up Lil man the fiend said? You remember me don't you Manny asked? Yea, you Brenda's boy right. Yea, look I'm sorry about how you caught me and ya moms, that's my buddy tho, the mark said. Man yall grown that shit ain't have nothing to do with me homie, Manny said. I gotta proposition for you tho, Manny said as the man

kept staring at him all crazy, fuck wrong with yo nigga, Manny said as he caught the dude looking at him like he saw something on his face. Shit, young blood I'm just tweaking right now, yall got some good shit over there he said, yea aight look tho, we doing a pass out tomorrow, for what, the fiend cut him off, yall shit already the bomb he said, yea I know but I'm tryna open up another spot in Englewood tho. I want you to tell all your people that we are doing a pass out in the alley behind the building, but we are going to open the spot up on the block in Englewood. We just wanna show them what we got, Manny said. Aight, youngin I got ya, I don't get the logic in it but I'll do it tho. Aight cool, here Manny said handing him a $100 bill. Damn, thanks shawty the fiend said about to walk off. Aye, meet me right in the front at 10 pm tonight. I'll give you a sample of what we will be handing out tomorrow, Manny said. Aight Lil homie, you ain't bullshtting is you, the fiend said. Does it look like I play games, Manny said. You right Lil man I'll be here at 9:59 on the dot the fiend said leaving out the building. Manny went up to his mama's apartment and the door was cracked open, he walked in and caught his mother in a deep nod. Manny walked up and smacked the fuck outta her knocking her outta the chair. What the fuck wrong with you she shouted as she jumped up. Don't ever put ya God damn hands on me, I'm still ya mama, despite what you think of me she snapped. You ain't tired of living like this mama, Manny whispered. I need you to stop doing this shit ma, I can take good care of you. I got many now, I can move you to any crib you want. It ain't too late to clean yourself up and get a job, Manny said, damn near in tears. I wanna stop but I can't. I'm hooked baby Brenda said with tears streaming down her cheeks. Just say the word and I'll help you get ya life together, manny said. Ok, come by here and see me tomorrow so we can talk. I can't really function right now off this shit, Brenda said. Alright, I'll be here early, with Alexandria Manny said. Aw, you finally stop being shy huh his mom said as he walked to the door to leave. I'll be here by 10 be woke, Manny said leaving out the door. Manny stood in front of the elevator, emotions all over the place, hoping that he'd broken through to his mom. As Manny got on the elevator, a smile appeared on his face, he had the perfect plan in place to get rid of the fiend witness. The doors opened up and Manny stepped out of the elevator, looked around, and walked back to the car. You saw him, Alex said when Manny got back into the car. Yup Manny replied, so why you ain't say shit we coulda grabbed the nigga and took care of that shit now, Alex said yelling. Be cool I got the perfect plan in place, Manny said. Bowie still got that bad dope with the fytenol on it, Manny asked. Hell yea, he put that shit in an abandoned car in the hood so the law wouldn't find it. That shit will kill a muthafucka right, Manny asked. Hell yea, that's why we ain't put it out, that shit killed 5 muthafuckas that we let test it chuck said. If that ain't strong enough I don't know what is. Aight bet, I need you to grab at least 2 grams of it and meet me right here at 9:30 tonight, Manny said. Aight cool, I'm finna grab it now and just put it in the slot upstairs until it's time, Chuck said. Ok cool, let me out on the corner, I'm finna post up with Lil folk nem, Manny said as they pulled up to the stop sign. HML, Manny said jumping out of the car.

Chuck and Alex hopped on the eway on 43rd heading to Englewood. I hope this nigga Manny knows what he doing, Alex said. Aw if that nigga snort this shit, he fasho dying I can vouch for that, Chuck said laughing. That shit that potent? Alex asked, nigga we did a pass out with the shit before we linked up with yall, and the first 5 fiends that tested it died in the bando on the block, Chuck said. The crazy thing about it, tho the fiends started coming even harder once they knew that shit was deadly, but Bowie anit wanna fuck with it because of all the police shit coming from it. I feel him, Alex said. As they hopped off the eway on 63rd. If that's not strong enough. I got something to put on it to make sure his ass check instantly, Chuck said as they passed morgan. Whatever we gotta do, we gotta make it happen for Big Dawg so he can come home, Alex replied. I'm already knowing, Chuck agreed. I wonder how it's gonna be when folks come home tho? Alex said, what you mean, Chuck replied? I'm saying when he left we were Lil nigga's working packs, he gave us the game and some bread to get right. We took the shit to another level with it and got super right, Alex said. What could he do besides get in line and accept what he got coming to him, Chuck said. It's a new day now, It's our turn. I know yall got a bag put up for'em and a position in the organization also, but if he thinks he finna be back running shit he a fucking fool and yall some fools if yall let him, Chuck snapped as he pulled up to the block. I'll be back, I'm finna grab this shit Chuck said jumping out leaving Alex thinking about what he said.

Chapter 20
(9:25 that night)

This nigga needs to come on, so I can go to the crib, Manny said as they stood in front of the building. Where you gone have the nigga snort the shit at Chuck asked. Shid, we gonna let'em sit in the back seat and hit it manny said. Aw ok, let the nigga die in my shit, huh Chuck replied. Where you want him to go upstairs to my crib and my O.G. hit the shit with him and both of'em die, Manny snapped, besides, we don't want the nigga to die in the building anyway making it hot, manny added. We let him do the shit in the car and once he checks out, we drive his ass somewhere and throw him out, Manny said. Yea aight smart ass, Chuck said. I think that's him right there, Manny said, looking up the block. Yea that's him. Youngblood,

~ 116 ~

what it do the hype says walking up? You got it, Manny said, shaking old skool hand, placing the dope in his palms at the same time. Aight blood, good lookin I'll be right with you the fiend said about to walk off. Naw old skool you can sit in the car and hit that shit, Manny said, we wanna see what it do, we gotta ride out, Manny added. Ok, ok, the hype said jumping in the back seat. Manny looked at Chuck like nigga this shit better do it, Chuck already knew what the look meant, he just nodded his head, with a devilish grin on his face. Manny heard the hype coughing and tapping the window. Manny just looked at him, watching the dope take over the hype body. He was in the backseat foaming at the mouth, grabbing his throat as if he couldn't breathe. Yea that shit finna knock his ass out, Chuck said. Seconds later he stopped moving and slumped in the back seat, he outta there, Chuck said, opening the door. Come on nigga he said to Manny as they both got in the car, where we gone take him, Manny said, Nigga any alley that ain't by the block. Matter of fact drop his ass by the D spot on 52nd Indiana, Manny said. Yup Chuck agreed as they drove down 47th street then turned up Indiana to see if the block was clear. When they got to 52nd manny looked around for any cameras on the poles. Ride down the alley first to see if any of the garages got cameras on'em, Manny said. Man, you tryna get us bumped,

Chuck said, cruising down the alley as Manny checked the garages. Aight we good Manny said, opening the door and pulling the hype out by his shoes, leaving him in the middle of the alley as they flew off. Damn, I should've at least put'em in the cut, Manny said. Hell yea, you could've given him a pillow and blanket too, Chuck said jokingly. You can tell this your first time around a dead nigga, Chuck added looking at Manny laughing to entire time as they drove toward Manny's crib, shut the fuck up and drop me off nigga, Manny snapped.

Chapter 21
Next Morning

It was 11:45 am when Manny woke up. Damn, he said to himself as he jumped up. Alexandria, Manny yelled, what bae, she responded from downstairs. Why the fuck you let me sleep so late, Manny said, cutting the shower on. I didn't know you had somewhere to be, Alexandria said, with her stomach protruding over her boy shorts, while throwing something on, we finna go holla at my O.G. and check her ass in a rehab, Manny said as he stood in the walk-in shower. Ok, Babe, she said as she undressed in the doorway. I said put some clothes on, not take clothes off. Shut up, I'm horny she said, stepping into the shower and sliding in from the back. Ooh, baby Alexandria said biting down on her bottom lip, as Manny pounded away from behind her. Damn, this pregnant pussy is so wet, Manny said in her ear. I love you, Bae, Alexandria said, as she felt herself about to cum. Damn baby I'm finna cum, Manny whispered in her ear, me too baby she said back. Manny pumps started to get short and stiff and he busts all in Alexandria. I came baby, Manny said, me too she said back as she grabbed the towel and washed Manny's back as he leaned his head up against the wall.

An hour later Alexandria was pulling up in front of the projects in her brand new X7. Come on, Manny said, jumping out heading to the building. Alexandria jumped out and grabbed Manny's hand as they walked into their old building. Damn, I'm glad we don't live here anymore she said as they got on the elevator. Who you telling, Manny replied. They got off the elevator on the 13th floor and walked to Manny's old apartment, like always the door was open. Manny walked in and with Alexandria right on his heels, Ma, Manny yelled, all he heard were sniffles. Ma where you at? Come out here, Manny said, walking to her bedroom. What are you crying for Ma? Manny asked. Brenda was clearly going through something because she never cried, not that Manny knew of. What's wrong Ma? Manny asked, walking up to her and sitting on the bed by her side. They found Eman dead in the alley, Brenda said, who da fuck is Eman, Manny said. The guy who you caught me in the room with, Brenda said. Aw him, Manny replied. Ok, going down this road that's bound to happen ma, that's what I'm tryna get you to see, Manny snapped. They said it was some bad dope that killed him as soon as it hit his bloodstream. I'm sorry Ma, I know that was yo friend, he was more than a friend, we came up together, went to school together. He was my first love, Brenda said, in between sobs. Her sobbing made Manny feel like the scum of the earth. I'm sorry Ma, but I need you to get dressed, I wanna put you in inpatient rehab, it's a 6-month program. The best in Illinois, you finish that, you can come and live with me and Dria. I gotta house with 8 bedrooms and you gotta grandbaby on the way.

Grandbabies, Alexandria jumped in, I'm having twins, a boy, and a girl. See Ma, you got grandbabies that need you, Manny said. Ok baby, Brend said, getting up out of the bed. I guess the death of Eman played a part in it, Manny said to himself. Usually, she would've told me to fuck off.

Alright Ma, you ain't gotta pack none of this shit. Just get what is important and leave the rest, besides what you are wearing. Dria will take you shopping to get you everything you need once we enroll you in the Rehab, Manny said. Alright, Brenda responded, let me get in the shower and then I'll be ready. 30 Minutes later Brenda, Alexandria, and Manny was getting into the X7. As they pulled off heading for the eway, Manny kept looking in the rearview at his mom. Something about her was all the way off. She was never this emotional, especially about a nigga on the street. The only nigga she told me she ever cried over was my daddy and that was when I was a newborn, Manny thought. Ma! Manny yelled, snapping Brenda out of her daydream, here Manny said, handing her a pamphlet to the rehab-ilitation center. They got everything on campus, we're gonna come see you every weekend too and you can call every day, so you'll never feel lonely, Manny said. It seems nice Brenda said dropping the pamphlet on the seat staring out the window. The GPS says we'll be there in five minutes, Alexandria said, aight Manny replied. Five minutes later they were walking into Helping Hands Rehab. Alexandria did all the talking and all the financial stuff too. After about 20 minutes of filling out the paperwork, they were done. Alright Ms. Montgomery you're all settled. Now, you can follow me, the Staff member said. Can you give us a sec, Manny asked, sure the lady responded. Ma, I want you to know that I'm proud of you and that I love you, we're here with you every step of the way, Manny said, dropping a tear. I love you too son and thank you for not giving up on me, Brenda said emotionally. I'll never give up on you Ma, Manny replied. Now Dria got your sizes and stuff, she's gone, drop you off a wardrobe tomorrow alright, Manny said. Ok baby, Brenda replied I'll see you this weekend and call me whenever you feel like it, Manny said, as the orderly took Brenda to her room.

Chapter 22

Alex, Chuck, and Short had just left the spot up north grabbing 20 bricks to take to the building. I don't know why yo ass wanted to come during rush hour, Short said. Because it's the best time to have all this shit on us. The Law ain't tryna pull no muthafucka over in all this traffic, Alex said. Yea aight, Short said, turning off

LakeShore on Chicago Ave, Because of all the traffic. Why the fuck you get off, Chuck said, I know a short cut, nigga be cool, Short said as he gassed it up Hubbard and turned on State Street. Out of nowhere, Alex saw the police on bikes flagging them to pull over, apparently Short turned in no turning lane. Man the law on us, Alex said. Where Short asked, on these bikes coming behind us, nigga you tweaking, Short said snatching off as the bikes approached them. You could tell that they had radioed in the car by how they grabbed their walkie-talkie. Short was flying through red lights and stop signs, but they were in a Toyota Avalon, wasn't any escaping that Motorolla today. Short tried to hop back on Lake Shore but a blue and white were coming from that way, so he had to reroute and go back up State Street. By this time he got to State Street a Tahoe and 3 blue and whites were coming down State Street and the blue and white that was coming from Lake Shore was behind him. They were boxed in all they could do is surrender or run, but run where? It was at least 30 cars surrounding them, now all they could do was take that L. The police walked up to the car snatching all the doors open and pulling all 3 occupants out face down on the ground. Thought you got away the 2 bikes police said as they rode up. Fuck you, bike boy, Chuck said. Aw, I see what you ass holes ran for, one of the officers said. These muthafuckas had a shit load of cocaine in the car with them, the police officer said grabbing the bag outta the car.

Take these muthafucas to 18th St, keep'em separate the Detective said. I'm right behind you.

20 minutes later the Detective came into the interrogation room where Alex was at. So what you thought you was finna get away from me, your Lil dumb ass. Aye look homie you about to sit here and waste every breath in yo body talking to me, so I' ma save you the time, gone charge me, process me, and send me to bond court homie. You got it all figured out huh, tell me who you got this shit from and you can walk right out the back no charges, no nothing. I see you 17 about to be 18 in a month or so, so you are definitely going to the County and that ain't no place for a first-timer, mark my words the Detective said. Alex sat there looking at him. The Detective doesn't know that Alex won't make it to a Deck. His paper was long as train smoke. Alright, have it your way dumb ass. Now when ya buddy rolls on you, you're going to try to cut a deal, but it'll be too

late. I'll have the last laugh tho he said walking out. The Detective must've had bad luck because Chuck told'em to suck his Dick and bring him his sandwich when the Detective walked in the room where he was. They couldn't talk to Short because he was only 15 so he needed a Juvenile Advocate there to speak for him, but he definitely was going back to St. Charles, he wasn't tripping, he knew as long as he told the Judge he was in school, he would be out in a month max. The Detective took Alex and Chuck in the back for processing then gave them a phone call. Alex called his sister, she recognized the number from all the times Alex called in the past. Hello, she said, Dria I got pulled over with some work on me, a lot, but I wasn't driving tho. I got bond court tomorrow at the county at 10 am, yall be there, tell Manny that Chuck and Short are with me, but Short is going to Juvenile and to be on point for us. Already, you know yall good Alexandria said, trying to keep her brother spirits up. Aight let's go, the turnkey said. You making a call he asked Chuck, Naw I'm good. Aight you two asshols are cellys for the night the turnkey said opening the cell and slamming the door behind them.

Bond Court

The state calls Alexander Smith and Charles Lee. Chuck and Alex came out the back looking in the stands to see who was out there for them and only saw Alexandria, shid that's cool. I know she got that bread on deck. Folks nem ain't have to show up, Alex said to himself. Whatever lawyer that was hired for them tho, she was a pit bull in a dress, as the state presented their case, they tried to make Chuck and Alex look like drug lords, But when their Attorney Ms. Clapp got through with her case the Judge damn near wanted to give them I bonds. Alright, alright I've heard both side arguments, but that amount of drugs that was seized was a lot, I grant both defendants bond set at $100,000 source bond with electronic monitoring next case. As they took Alex and Chuck to the back the lawyer followed back also. Hey, I was sent by a friend of yours, who's a friend of a friend, if you know what I mean. Yea we know, Alex said. While we were prepared for this already, so as we speak

I have someone drawing up papers for appraisals for the both of you. I'll have that done by tomorrow evening and on the Judge's desk the next day. So unfortunately you guys will have to sit a day or 2 in the County Jail. But everything already paid for, once the paper is done you're out, the lawyer said aight. I guess we gotta sit then, Alex said. Aw and your sister said to call her too when you can Ms. Clapp, said walking off.

Chapter 23

On the new, the deck worker hollered as Chuck and Alex came through the door. Alexander, you're in cell 10 top bunk, and Charles you're in 6 lower bunk the C/O said as he popped the door from the desk. When Chuck entered the cell his celly was doing pushups, where you from homie he asked Chuck. I'm from Willieville in Englewood Chuck said. Aw ok, I've been hearing y'all name ringing out there. You boys getting a lot of money. What the fuck is y'all doing here? He said. I'm not finna be here blood, just waiting on them to get the paperwork together for the appraisal Chuck said. Aw ok then, that shit can take a while, depending on your lawyer, his celly said. I gotta dog, she's already on top of it, I'll be outta here by Saturday, Chuck said. I already know, his celly said. Whatever you need I got it as far as hygiene or food. I'm finna go home in a couple of weeks, his celly said. Aight bet, I'm tired as hell tho, I'm finna go to sleep. I'll holla at you in the AM, Chuck said, getting on his bunk. When Alex got into his cell, it was pitch black. His celly was asleep. Alex turned the light on so he could get his stuff situated and his celly started moving as if the light had woke him up, man, what the fuck his celly said, removing the blanket from off his head. Aye bro you gone have to wait till the AM to do that shit. I got court in the morning, his celly said. Man, I don't give no fuck what you got in the morning I gotta get my bunk in order, so I can K.O., Alex said. What nigga his celly said, now jumping outta the bed. Who the fuck you, Miguel was at a loss for words when he saw his Lil man, Alex standing in front of him. Alex, Miguel said. I can't believe this shit, Miguel said. Big homie what's up, Alex said? Shit man, Miguel said, pulling Alex in for a hug. Damn, I ain't saw yo ass in a minute, Miguel said. I ain't heard shit but good things about you lil niggas,

Miguel said. You know we had to hold it down for you big dawg, Alex boosted. They say yall getting to it out there, Miguel said. I ain't gone lie, we branched off all into Englewood. We got the whole hood over there on lock. Lil Sam's cousin Bowie got it sowed up. Ain't shit moving thru there unless he says so and we all on one team so you already know wassup they said. Miguel couldn't do shit but smile. So how the fuck y'all get in here? We got bumped with 20 bricks coming from your slot, Alex said. My man Chuck in cell 10, he from Willieville too. Straight killer tho, me, him, and my other Lil Man Short got pulled over. Short a Juvenile tho, so he went to the auddy home. Our bond and shit already taken care of, it was a $100,000 source bond, the lawyer already got everything in order, she said we'll be out in a couple of days, Alex informed Miguel. Aight, aight what happened with the other thing. I haven't talked to anybody yet, I was gonna call at 1 am. 1 am how the fuck you gone do that, Alex said. Miguel got up, went to his stash, and pulled out a flip phone, this how nigga. Aw I see you fool, but we took care of that, you finna be a free man homie, Alex said. That's what's up Lil homie. I'm proud of you niggas, for a real man. I hope y'all left some room for me, Miguel joked. Come on Big homie! You already know wassup, Alex replied and you got a big bag of money waiting on you too, Alex said. Miguel couldn't do shit but smile. They sat up all night talking about everything that had been going on in the hood, by the time they were done talking the C/O was popping the door, time for court Miguel.

Chapter 24

Miguel sat in the courtroom, behind the big cherry oak wood desk with his eyes locked on the judge. You two approach the bench, the judge told Miguel's lawyer and the prosecutor. Miguel's stomach was doing summersaults as the 2 attorneys stood in front of the Judge. Where's your witness the Judge asked the prosecutor, I'm sorry your honor my Investigator hasn't tracked him down yet. If you can give me another status date by agreement with the attorney, I'm sure I can have him here within another month. A month the lawyer said, so you expect my client to sit in jail rotting away just because you can't find your witness. Your Honor my client has been in jail without a bond for almost a year and a half, forbidden from seeing his young child that he just had, due to covid-19 and any of his other family members for that matter. I am submitting a motion to dismiss all charges against my client. I agree Ms. Clapp the judge said as she sent the 2 attorneys back to their desk. Unfortunately, the State can't prove beyond a reasonable doubt that the defendant has committed the crimes he's charged with because they can't find their witness, so I have no choice but to grant the defense motion to dismiss all charges, Bailiff please take Mr. Santos back to the jail, so he can be processed out. Next case. The Bailiff walked Miguel to Division 9. Miguel was in awe, he thought he was for sure booked when he first caught the case. He did a solid for his Lil 'mans and they returned the favor. Miguel was all smiles as he walked through the doors on his deck, everybody rushed him asking him what had happened. You know they found ya boy not guilty, Miguel said lying like he actually went to trial, come on the C/O said annoyed that Miguel was about to be free. He popped Miguel's cell, so he could get all his shit together. When he walked in, Alex was sitting on the bed shuffling a deck of cards. I see everything worked out huh, Alex said jumping down. Hell yea, Love Lil homie, I'll be seeing you tomorrow when you come home, Miguel said. Here, the charger in the cell with my man in cell 3, you ain't gonna need it anyway Miguel said, as he gave Alex the flip phone. As long as the C/O ain't on the deck you good to use it otherwise wait until after count Miguel informed him. Aight I' ma just give yo man the phone when they let me out tomorrow, Alex said. Aight I'm gone my nigga, Miguel said as he walked out of the cell. Aw yeah, I'm back Miguel said in the dayroom. The takeover about to start as we speak he added walking off the Deck. Alex pulled out the phone and dialed Manny's cell. Manny picked up right away knowing that it was Miguel's burner. What's up big homie, Manny said into the receiver. Naw nigga this Alex, Alex how the fuck you get Miguel's phone, Manny said. Cus he was my celly Alex replied, was your celly, where he at? Manny asked. He went to trial today and they threw the case out because they couldn't find the witness,

Alex said. Aw ok, that's love, it's finna be cracking, manny said. I'm already knowing, Alex said. I ain't on shit tho, I was just telling you ya mans was coming home. My mans, I thought you would be the main one excited, Manny said. I am but I ain't feeling the nigga vibe tho, I just don't trust him for some reason, I think he gotta hidden agenda, he just gave me the wrong vibe bro, but I might be tweaking tho, Alex said. Yea, I think you tweaking, ain't no reason for fool to be on no sneaky shit. He put us on and finna come home to a bag of money so I don't know, you might just not be feeling that jail shit, that's all, Manny said. You right gone head and do yo thang tho, I'm finna rap with Chuck and wait for them to call our names tomorrow, Alex said. That's a fact, love bro, Manny replied, hanging up.

I'm here for Brenda Montgomery, Manny said to the receptionist. I'm her son Emmanuel Potts and this is my girlfriend Alexandria Wilson. The receptionist looked on the computer to see they were on the visiting list. Ok right this way she said as she ushered them to Brend's room. There she is, the lady said opening the door to Brenda's room. You have a blessed day she said walking off. Brenda sat in the chair staring out the window not even noticing that Manny and Alexandria came into the room. Ma, Manny said, snapping her out the deep train of thought she was in. Yea son, Brenda said, sniffing due to her crying. Why you crying ma, Alexandria said. Because I'm a horrible woman that lies and cheats, I should be dead instead of him, Brenda said, referring to Eman. Ma, he was just a nigga on the street, ok yall went way back, but it's time to move on, he made his decisions in life and it caught up with him, Manny said not showing any remorse knowing that it was his fault that Eman was dead. It's not that simple son, Brenda said, sit down for a second she told Manny. Manny sat on the edge of her bed, holding his mother's hand. What's the real problem Ma, you can tell me, Manny said. Well, baby, I lied about why your father left us, what you mean Manny replied. He didn't leave us because he didn't want kids, in fact, he loved you and wanted to be the best father he could be, so what happened? Manny asked. I cheated on him while I was pregnant with you and I got caught up with the other guy so your father thought that the baby was the other guy's baby. I took a DNA test and everything to prove to your father that he was your Dad, but the damage was done already. He didn't want anything to do with us anymore, so I lied to you and told you that he walked out on us, when in fact everything was my fault, Brenda said crying. Why are you telling me all this shit now, Manny said, furious with his mom. Because that man you caught me with, in the room that day, the man that they found in the alley dead, he was your father. My father, what the fuck you mean he was my father, Manny snapped? After he left us, he got strung out on drugs, and years later he started coming back around, but it wasn't no use in telling you then because he was strung out on drugs. His name is Emmanuel Potts, your name is Emmanuel Potts Jr, Manny. Eman is short for Emmanuel, Brenda said. That's why he was staring at me in the hallway that day, Manny said. I can't believe you Ma, I can't, let's go Alexandria, but hold on, Bae let her finish. I said let's go, Manny said, raising his voice.

Alexandria jumped out and headed for the door. Ma, you're dead to me, Manny said walking outta the door leaving Brenda speechless.

To Be Continued

Part Two Coming Soon!!!

About the Author

Jamar Jenkins Chicago, IL.

Jamar Jenkins Author of Domino Effect now brings his new novel The Corner. Jamar enjoys writing and spending time with his two sons, his sister, his niece & nephews, and his friends. Jamar is eager to continue his writing career with sequels to both Domino Effect and The Corner and hopes to also include more novels in his series.

Made in the USA
Monee, IL
24 July 2021

73793578R00085